Little Star

Carefully Neil picked Star out of the huddle of puppies and cradled her on his lap. She was so tiny – a ball of white fluff small enough to rest in his hand, her eyes still tightly closed. Her fur was damp and frizzy where Willow had been cleaning her. She whimpered softly. Emily held the feeding bottle against Star's tiny lips, but she turned her head away . . .

Titles in the Puppy Patrol® series

More Puppy Patrol® stories to follow soon

Puppy Patrol®
Little Star

Jenny Dale

Illustrated by

Mick Reid

A Working Partners Book

MACMILLAN CHILDREN'S BOOKS

Special thanks to Cherith Baldry

First published 2001 by Macmillan Children's Books
a division of Pan Macmillan Limited
20 New Wharf Road, London N1 9RR
Basingstoke and Oxford
www.panmacmillan.com

Associated companies throughout the world

Created by Working Partners Limited
London W6 0QT

ISBN 0 330 39844 X

1 3 5 7 9 8 6 4 2

A CIP catalogue record for this book is available from
the British Library.

Typeset in Bookman Old Style by SX Composing DTP, Rayleigh, Essex
Printed and bound in Great Britain by Mackays of Chatham plc, Kent

Chapter One

"**C**ome on, Em!" Neil Parker stopped outside the door of Meadowbank School and waited impatiently for his sister. "I want to get home and walk Jake before it gets dark."

Neil's breath billowed out in a cloud in the frosty air. A thin dusting of snow covered the playground, and the grey sky threatened more snow to come. Neil pulled his cap down over his spiky brown hair and stamped his feet to keep warm. "Come *on!*" he repeated.

Emily, Neil's ten-year-old sister, was struggling with a rolled-up poster, her bulging school bag, and a papier mâché donkey she'd made for her class's Christmas crib. "I'm

1

coming," she said. "I've got tons of things to take home." A huge smile spread across her face. "I can't wait for Christmas!"

"I know." Neil grinned in return. "And no more school for three whole weeks. Just dogs, all day and every day!"

Neil and Emily's parents, Bob and Carole Parker, ran King Street Kennels and rescue centre, just outside the little country town of Compton. Neil and his family loved dogs so much that Neil's friends called them the Puppy Patrol.

As he and Emily hurried down the side of the school towards the bike sheds, Neil thought about Jake, his young Border collie. He imagined days and days playing together in the exercise field behind the house, or up on the ridgeway. Not to mention lots of training sessions in the barn.

Just as they approached the corner by the rubbish bins, they heard a dog begin to bark. A small child started to wail loudly.

"Oh no! I wonder what's going on?" said Emily.

Neil frowned. "I don't recognize that bark. It's definitely not Dotty." Dotty was the excitable Dalmatian owned by Mr Hamley, Neil's headteacher.

They ran even faster. As they turned the corner, they saw a small boy from the infants' class. He was howling, with his eyes screwed up and the contents of his bag scattered at his feet.

Julie Baker, from Emily's class, was kneeling down beside the little boy. She was trying to comfort him, while Neil's best friend, Chris Wilson, was peering nervously at something behind the dustbins.

The barking had turned into a low growling noise, but Neil couldn't see what was making it. "What is it?" he asked.

"It's a strange dog," Julie said. She sounded scared. "Come and look, Neil."

As Neil went over to the dustbins, one of them crashed over, spilling rubbish out onto the playground. A big dog appeared from behind the bin, pushed his head into the rubbish, and started rooting hungrily through the discarded food wrappers.

The dog had a smooth black coat with tan markings around his face and on his paws. His ears were pointed and he had a short, stumpy tail. *A Doberman*, thought Neil. He knew they could be aggressive if they weren't handled properly.

"What happened?" Emily asked. She dumped

her things on the ground and went to help Julie look after the little boy.

"The dog was just hanging about," Chris explained. "Mark went up to pat him, and the dog snarled at him and grabbed his bag."

"Did he bite him?" Emily asked anxiously. She gave the little boy a gentle smile. "Mark, did the dog hurt you?"

Mark shook his head. He was starting to calm down. "He took my chocolate," he sobbed, pointing to an empty chocolate bar wrapper.

Emily let out a sigh of relief.

Neil went over to Mark and stood looking down at him. "You should never try to pat a strange dog," he explained kindly. "You probably frightened him."

"Trust you, Neil!" Chris exclaimed, with a grin. "It's never the dog's fault, is it?"

"There are no problem dogs, only problem owners," Neil said, repeating something his dad was always saying. "What's this one doing here, that's what I'd like to know."

He turned back to the dog, which had pulled a half-eaten sandwich out of the bin and was wolfing it down ravenously. Neil realized that he was quite a young dog. His dark coat, which should have been sleek and glossy, looked dull and uncared for, and he was so thin that all his ribs were showing. A heavy studded collar hung loosely round his neck.

"He's been living rough for a while," Neil said. "Just look at him!"

The dog finished the sandwich and looked round, flattening his ears and letting out a growl from deep in his throat.

"Neil, come away," Julie said nervously.

"It's OK," Neil reassured her. "The dog won't attack us if we don't bother him."

He looked round to see that several more of his friends had come up and were standing around uncertainly, looking at the strange dog.

"Just walk past quietly," Neil directed them. "He's not dangerous if you don't scare him."

He waited until the others had gone, and then carefully took a step towards the dog. At once it lowered its head, and the growling grew louder and more threatening.

"Neil, don't," Emily said. "We need to fetch Dad."

"OK," Neil agreed. He had to admit that he didn't fancy tackling the dog by himself. "You go – I'll keep an eye on the dog."

Emily collected Mark's scattered belongings and put them back in his bag. Then she took the little boy's hand. "We'll go to the infants' playground and find Mark's mum," she said. "I bet Dad will be there too, picking up Sarah." She led Mark off, round the side of the school.

"Don't let Sarah come round here!" Neil called after her. He knew how their five-year-old sister insisted on cuddling all the dogs that came to King Street. This dog didn't look cuddly at all.

Chris and Julie went to the shed to fetch their bikes, while Neil stood watching the dog. It had started pawing through the contents of the bin again.

He couldn't remember anyone phoning the

kennels to ask about a lost Doberman, but he hoped that somewhere a frantic owner was trying to trace their pet. Thank goodness the dog had an identity disc on his collar, thought Neil. He was pretty sure the dog could soon be reunited with his owner.

A few minutes later Bob Parker strode round the corner, dangling a muzzle and lead from one hand. Bob was a big man, with broad shoulders and a bushy brown beard. He wore a green sweatshirt with the King Street Kennels logo on it. "What's all this?" he asked.

"Chris said the dog was just hanging about," Neil told him. "He seems really hungry."

"It looks like he's been homeless for quite a while," Bob said, studying the dog thoughtfully. "Look how thin he is! But he looks pretty well bred." He took a pace or two towards the dog, with one hand held out. Calmly, he said, "Here, boy. Steady. Come here."

The dog had been sniffing an empty yoghurt carton but, as Bob spoke, his head whipped up. He snarled, baring strong white teeth. Cautiously Bob moved closer but the dog lunged at him, snapping.

"Dad!" Neil exclaimed in alarm.

Bob kept calm, but he stopped moving

forward. "OK. OK, boy," he said soothingly. "Neil, just get his attention a minute, will you? But don't startle him."

Neil nodded, trying to keep as calm as his dad. He clapped his hands together twice, and called, "Hey, boy! Here!"

The Doberman's head swung round. At once, Bob Parker stepped forward and grabbed the dog's collar. He let out a furious bark and began to struggle wildly, paws skidding on the ground, while Bob clipped the muzzle into place.

Neil darted forward to help.

"No, Neil – keep back!" Bob warned.

Neil stopped and watched anxiously as the

snapping jaws were held safely in the muzzle and the strap was fastened.

"There," Bob said with a sigh of relief. He stood up, keeping a grip on the Doberman's collar as he clipped on the lead.

"Let me see if I can read his identity disc," said Neil. He walked slowly up to the dog and bent down.

Though the dog tried to pull away, Neil managed to get hold of the disc. "There's a phone number," he told his dad. "A Padsham number, I think. And it says his name's Brutus."

"Great," said Bob. He stroked the Doberman's head. "That means we should be able to trace his owner."

"Come on, Brutus," Neil said, straightening up. "Let's try to have you home for Christmas!"

Back at King Street Kennels, Bob took Brutus to the rescue centre while Neil tried ringing the number on the disc but there was only the shrill drawn-out tone which meant the number was unobtainable.

Neil sighed with disappointment. Reuniting Brutus with his owner wasn't going to be as easy as he had thought.

Replacing the receiver, he went out to the rescue centre, where he found Bob and Emily settling Brutus into his pen. Bob had already asked Emily to put down bowls of food and water. Cautiously, he led Brutus into the pen and unclipped the muzzle. This time Brutus didn't try to attack him. He made straight for the water bowl and took a long drink.

"He'll be fine," Bob said, as he came out of the pen and fastened the door. "But you're not to go into the pen with him until we're sure he's settled down."

"OK," said Neil. He watched as Brutus wolfed down the food in the bowl and then flopped down with his nose on his paws.

"He's tired out," said Emily. "Poor thing, he must have been wandering round for ages."

"Did you manage to get hold of his owner?" Bob asked.

Neil shook his head and explained that the number on the disc had been unobtainable.

"I'll ring Sergeant Moorhead," Bob said. "And Terri McCall at the RSPCA. Somebody might have reported Brutus missing."

He strode out of the rescue centre. Neil and Emily stayed watching Brutus for a minute or two more, before checking on the other rescue dogs. There were only two others: a perky black mongrel, and a young bull terrier who was watching them bright-eyed through the mesh of the pen.

Neil fed them dog treats from the supply he always kept in his pockets. Luckily both dogs had already been visited by several families who wanted to take them, and Neil was confident they would be in new homes by Christmas. He wondered if Brutus would be so lucky.

Neil and Emily left the rescue centre and hurried across to the house. It was growing dark, and the snow was falling more steadily, covering the courtyard with a layer of white.

Inside, the kitchen was warm and filled with tempting smells of supper. Carole Parker was standing at the cooker, stirring something in a pan. As Neil opened the door, Jake, his young Border collie, leapt up from his basket in the corner and bounded over to him, barking delightedly.

"Hi, Jake!" Neil said, bending over to ruffle the dog's ears. "Mum, I haven't had time to walk Jake. Can I take him out now?"

"No, supper's nearly ready," said Carole. "And it's dark outside. Don't worry, I gave him a run earlier, before it started snowing too heavily."

"Snow for Christmas!" Neil's little sister Sarah was bouncing up and down at the big kitchen table where she was pasting strips of coloured paper together to make a chain. "I'm going to show Fudge how to make a snowman."

Neil groaned. Sarah thought that Fudge, her hamster, was clever enough to do anything.

"It's far too cold for Fudge outside," said Carole. "Let him stay in his nice warm cage."

"But Fudge *wants* to make a snowman," Sarah protested.

"No, he doesn't, he's only a hamster," said Neil impatiently. He was still feeling worried that he hadn't been able to contact Brutus's owner.

"Mum!" Sarah's voice rose to a wail. "Neil said—"

"Never mind, Sarah," Emily interrupted quickly. "Tomorrow we'll make a snow hamster together. And Fudge can look at it through the window."

Sarah thought about that for a moment and beamed happily.

"What's for supper?" Neil asked his mum. "I'm as hungry as Brutus!"

"Chilli and rice. Wash your hands, you two,

12

and, Sarah, clear your things off the table."

Neil was at the sink in the utility room when his dad came out of the office.

Bob was shaking his head. "The police haven't had any reports of a lost Doberman," he said. "Not here or in Padsham. Neither have the RSPCA." He went over to the cooker, stirred the pot of rice and unhooked a sieve from the wall to drain it. "Maybe we'll have Brutus with us over Christmas after all," he added.

"His owner must be really worried," said Emily, getting knives and forks out of the kitchen drawer.

Neil knew she was right. He glanced down at Jake who was sitting beside the table with a hopeful look on his face. He knew how bad he would feel if he had to spend Christmas without his beloved dog. "We know Brutus's owner lives in Padsham," he said. "It can't be that difficult to find him." He finished drying his hands and came to sit down. "I'm going to try," he announced. "I'll get Brutus home for Christmas if it's the last thing I do!"

Chapter Two

B ob brought the pots of food to the table and everyone sat down. Neil took a forkful of the chilli that Carole spooned on to his plate. "I'll take a picture of Brutus and put it on the website," he decided.

"And tomorrow I'll phone Jake Fielding and see if he'll put something in the *Compton News*," Emily added. Jake Fielding was a photographer for the local paper and had covered several King Street stories in the past.

"And I'll make lots of posters!" said Sarah.

"A couple of posters would be a good idea," Bob said. "One in Mike Turner's surgery and one over at Jill Walker's – the vet in Padsham."

"Great!" said Neil. "And then we can—"

A knock at the kitchen door interrupted him. Carole got up to open it and Jake gave a welcoming bark as Kate and Glen Paget came in, brushing snow off their coats.

Kate was one of the Parkers' full-time kennel maids but she wasn't working at the moment because she was expecting a baby. Her fair hair was tucked under a brightly striped bobble hat and she wore a matching sweater.

"Kate!" said Carole. "Come in and sit down. How are you?"

Kate patted the bump under her sweater. "Huge," she said, smiling. "And pretty tired. I'll be glad when it's all over."

She sank down into the chair Bob brought for her. Her dog, a pretty Westie cross called Willow, waddled across the kitchen and sat down at her feet. Willow was expecting pups and looked just as big and uncomfortable as her owner.

"Willow will be glad when it's all over too," said Kate's husband Glen. "We'll have our hands full soon, with a new baby *and* a litter of pups!"

"I'm really glad that you can take Willow," said Kate. "I can't give her the attention she needs right now and Glen is out all day."

"Hey!" Neil exclaimed, jumping up from the table. "What do you mean, take Willow? What's going on that I don't know about?" He hoped nothing was wrong with the lively little dog – or Kate.

"Sit down and finish your supper," Carole said. She took her own place again, while Bob put the kettle on to make tea for Kate and Glen. "Kate rang me this afternoon. I forgot to tell you, what with everything else that's going on."

"Like Kate says, she can't give Willow the proper pre-whelping care just now," Bob explained. "She has to rest and make sure her baby's all right. So she asked us if we would look after Willow for the next few days."

"And of course we said yes," Carole finished.

"I'll come and see Willow every day," said Kate, "but I know she'll be fine here. She loves being with all of you – and Jake."

Jake had trotted over to Willow and was nosing her curiously. The dogs were good friends. Neil guessed that the Border collie was wondering why Willow wouldn't roll around with him as she usually did.

"We love having her," said Carole.

Neil exchanged a glance with Emily. They grinned at each other.

16

"Brill!" said Emily. "We'll have puppies for Christmas!"

"Puppies! Puppies!" said Sarah, wriggling on her chair and nearly knocking over her glass of orange juice. "Will they be born on Christmas Day?"

"They could be," said Glen. "I reckon it's going to be quite a race whether Willow has her pups or Kate has our baby first!"

When supper was over, Neil and Emily went across to the store room to fetch the whelping box. This was a box specially made for dogs about to give birth. It had high, protective sides and an infra-red heat lamp to keep the young pups warm. They carried it into the utility room and set it down in the corner furthest from the door, away from any cold draughts.

"We need newspapers to line the bottom," Neil said.

"There are loads in the cupboard under the stairs," said Emily. "I'll fetch some."

When she came back, Willow came waddling after her. The little dog sniffed the whelping box curiously as Emily lined the bottom with a thick layer of newspaper. "There you are, Willow," she said. "Nice and cosy."

Neil squatted down beside Willow and fished out a titbit for her. She snuffled it up, and gave him a happy look from bright eyes under shaggy white fur. Neil stroked her ears. "You'll be just fine here, girl," he promised her. "Real five-star service from the Puppy Patrol!"

Willow began to investigate the whelping box. Neil was tempting her into the box with some dog treats when Kate appeared in the doorway, with Glen behind her.

"This looks great," she said. "I know Willow's going to be fine." Awkwardly she bent over and gave her dog a farewell pat. "Be a good girl for Neil and Emily, do you hear?"

Willow looked up at Kate, wagging her stumpy tail, and gave her hand a swift lick. When Kate went back to the door, the little dog started to follow.

"No, girl," Neil said, taking hold of Willow's collar. "You've got to stay here."

"It won't be for long," Glen said. Neil wasn't sure whether he was trying to comfort Kate or Willow. They both looked sad to be saying goodbye.

As the door of the utility room closed behind Kate and Glen, Willow barked sharply. She stood still for a moment, whining, and then climbed into the whelping box, turned round a couple of times and settled down with her nose on her paws, watching the door intently.

Emily leant over to give her a reassuring stroke. "Kate will come and see you," she said, "and you'll be back home before you know it."

Willow's eyes stayed fixed on the door as if she was waiting for Kate to return. Watching the sad little dog, Neil resolved to give their Christmas visitor the best care that King Street Kennels had to offer.

As soon as he got up the next morning, Neil grabbed his digital camera and went downstairs. The kitchen was empty except for Jake in his basket. The young Border collie sprang up and went to stand beside the kitchen door as soon as he saw Neil, his plumy tail waving wildly.

"OK, boy," Neil said. "Hang on a minute."

Quietly he opened the door of the utility room to look in on Willow. The little white dog was curled up asleep in the whelping box and didn't stir as Neil peered at her round the door. He reached in and took down his jacket.

"Fine," Neil murmured, and closed the door again.

When he let Jake out, he saw that more snow had fallen in the night, covering the courtyard with a fluffy white blanket. Frost sparkled on the surface in the early morning sun.

Already, lines of footprints criss-crossed the courtyard. As Neil fastened his jacket, he saw his dad emerge from Red's Barn with an armful of bedding and plod through the snow towards Kennel Block One.

"Morning, Dad!" Neil called. "I'm going to take Brutus's picture."

"Don't go in the pen, OK?" Bob called back. "I'll be with you in a minute."

"Right!" Neil crunched across the snow,

20

heading for the rescue centre. Jake danced around him, barking joyfully and kicking up snow as he bounded across the yard. Neil shivered as the icy flakes caught him in the face. "Steady on, you daft dog!" he muttered.

Inside the rescue centre he found Bev, the Parkers' other full-time kennel maid, making up the morning feeds for the rescue dogs. She was a small, slender woman with a lively face. She was wearing jeans tucked into wellington boots and a sheepskin body warmer over a thick sweater. "Hi," she said. "You're up early."

"I want to take Brutus's picture, to put on the website," Neil explained. "Have you met Brutus? Isn't he a beauty?"

"He's a lovely dog," Bev agreed, pausing to take a look at the Doberman. Brutus was standing near the door of the pen, watching them through the mesh. "But your dad said he's unpredictable. He told me not to open the pen until he gets here."

"Last night he was hungry and scared, that's all. He'll be fine when he settles down," Neil said, leaping to Brutus's defence.

Jake appeared in the doorway and gave himself a vigorous shake, showering icy drops over Neil and Bev. Then he trotted over to

Brutus's pen and sniffed cautiously at the Doberman. Brutus lowered his head and the two dogs stood nose to nose.

"Hey, he likes Jake!" said Neil. He went over to the pen, but as soon as Brutus saw him he retreated a couple of paces.

"Steady, boy," Neil said. He fished a dog treat out of his pocket and gave it to Jake and then pushed another titbit through the mesh in front of Brutus.

The Doberman eyed it suspiciously before darting forward to snatch it up. He took it to the back of the pen to eat.

"Good boy," said Neil. "Come on, have another one." He pushed a second titbit through the mesh.

Still looking wary, Brutus padded over to take it.

"You're doing fine, boy," Neil said. "It won't be long before—"

Cold air wafted in behind him as the door opened. Brutus snarled, showing his sharp white teeth. He lowered his head threateningly and took a couple of steps backwards, stiff-legged.

Neil stared at the dog in alarm, then turned round to see what had upset him so much.

In the doorway stood his dad.

Chapter Three

"Dad!" Neil exclaimed. He couldn't understand it. Bob Parker was better at looking after dogs than anyone Neil had ever known. Neil couldn't believe that Brutus had changed so much, just at the sight of him.

"I hope you're being careful," Bob said. He shook his head sadly as he looked at the Doberman who was still growling fiercely at the back of his pen. "I had hoped he would be settling down by now."

"But he is," Neil protested. "At least, he was."

"That's right," said Bev, who had been watching Brutus closely. "Honestly, Bob, he was nervous with Neil, but not like *this*."

24

"He was fine until . . ." Neil's voice trailed off.

"Until I came in," Bob finished for him.

Neil nodded.

For a moment, Bob looked upset at the thought that any dog would be frightened of him. But then he shrugged. "Well," he said, "I'm the big ogre who put the muzzle on him. He might need time to get over that. All the same," he added, "*I'm* going to put the food in his pen, not you."

He took the bowls of food and water that Bev had already prepared. Neil opened the pen door. Brutus didn't move as Bob went in and put the bowls down, but he went on growling with a low, throaty sound. He didn't try to take the food until Bob had backed out of the pen and Neil had closed the door again.

"There must be something we can do for him until we find his owner," Neil said.

Bob nodded. "We'll do the best we can. Dobermans are wonderful dogs – loyal and intelligent, and not afraid of anything. Usually. Something bad must have happened to this one. The first thing he'll have to learn is to trust people again."

"You can trust us," Neil said to Brutus. "We'll look after you."

Once he had seen that Brutus was eating his breakfast, Bob went out again. Bev fed the other two rescue dogs and started to clear up the work area. "I'm off," she said when she had finished. "There are two new dogs coming in this morning, and I need to clean out the pens in Kennel Block One."

"I'll come and help you after breakfast," Neil said. He knew Bev had to work harder than ever now that Kate wasn't here. "But I want to take a picture of Brutus first, to put on the website."

"Thanks," said Bev. "I could do with another pair of hands. The first person to invent a self-cleaning dog pen will make a fortune!" She opened the door and looked back at Neil as she left. "Remember what your dad said. Don't open that door."

When he had taken a picture of Brutus, Neil went back to the house for breakfast. Bob was at the cooker, frying bacon and sausages, while Carole sorted through the morning post. Emily and Sarah were sitting at the table eating cereal.

Willow was awake now, sitting at Bob's feet with her eyes fixed on the pan. Jake bounded over to Willow and touched noses with her.

"I'm starving," Neil said, pulling off his jacket and stamping his feet on the mat to get rid of the slushy snow.

"Did you take Brutus's picture?" Emily asked him. "I'm going to update the website after breakfast."

Neil nodded, sliding into his place at the table and pouring himself a bowl of cereal. There were several envelopes beside his bowl.

"Christmas cards!" he said, tearing open the envelopes and spooning cereal into his mouth at the same time. "There's one with an American stamp – it must be from Jane and Richard."

The Parkers' neighbours, Jane and Richard Hammond, had recently left Compton to go and live in the United States. In the summer, Neil and Emily had visited them and their Border collie Delilah, who was Jake's mum.

"Yes, it is," Neil went on. "Oh, and there's another card inside – just look at that!"

He held out the card for Emily to see. On the front of it was a black-and-white dog wearing a Santa Claus hat, and inside it said, 'To Jake with love from Mum'. Beside the writing was a paw print. It was from Delilah.

"Hey, Jake, you've got a Christmas card!" said Emily.

Jake took no notice. He was far more interested in the bacon and sausages that Bob was dishing onto plates.

"I'm going to make a card for Fudge," Sarah announced.

"Good idea," said Emily. She gave Neil a sharp nudge with her elbow. "And then we're going to make a snow hamster, aren't we, Neil?"

"Can't," Neil mumbled through a mouthful of cornflakes. "I said I'd help Bev."

"Excuses, excuses," Emily said, grinning at him.

"Well, whatever you do, make sure you're finished by lunchtime," Carole said. "This afternoon we're all going to Padsham. You should be able to finish your Christmas shopping there."

"Oh, Mum, do we have to?" Neil protested. "There's loads to do here."

"Yes, you do," said Carole firmly. She started to collect the empty cereal bowls. "Unless you've bought every single present you need to buy. Tomorrow's Christmas Eve, so this is your last chance."

"OK, OK," Neil said. He began wolfing down his bacon, pausing only to slip scraps to Jake and Willow under the table. "Come on, Em.

Let's get to work on the website."

In the office Neil put the picture of Brutus up on the King Street Kennels' website, and then Emily typed in a description of the Doberman and the details of where he had been found. "You know," she said, with her fingers poised above the keyboard, "I'm not so sure about this."

"What do you mean?" Neil asked.

"Well . . . do we really *want* to find Brutus's owner? Look how scared and wild he is – maybe he's like that because his owner treated him badly."

"You don't know that," Neil argued. "He might have been fine until he got lost."

Emily shrugged and started typing again. "Maybe." She didn't sound convinced. "But if somebody does come to claim Brutus, I think we should check up really carefully before we hand him over."

Neil had to admit that his sister was right. Something had made Brutus mistrustful and angry. Neil wouldn't be satisfied until they found out what it was.

By lunchtime, Neil had helped Bev clean out the pens for the new arrivals, built a whole family of snow hamsters with Emily and Sarah and taken some of the boarding dogs for a run in the exercise field. By the time he returned the last of them, a highly excitable Cocker Spaniel, to its pen, he reckoned he deserved his lunch.

As Neil opened the kitchen door he almost tripped over Willow, who was peering out. "No, girl," he said, nudging her gently back inside with one foot. "It's far too cold for you out there. You stay in the warm and look after those pups!" He bent down and rubbed her swollen belly.

"She's been a bit restless this morning,"

Carole said, looking up from the copy of the *Compton News* she had spread over the kitchen table. "I think she's missing Kate and Glen. Your dad rang Mike Turner and he's going to come and give her the once-over later on."

"Great," said Neil. He peeled off his wet, woolly gloves. His fingers were so cold he could hardly feel them and he rubbed them together vigorously. "We'll look after you, Willow. Don't you worry about a thing."

Almost as if she understood him, Willow perked up a little and her stumpy tail started wagging. She trotted across the kitchen and buried her nose in her water bowl.

"I'm sure she's fine really," Carole said, "but—" She broke off as the kitchen door crashed open and Emily hurtled in. "Emily!"

"Sorry, Mum." Emily waved a piece of paper she was clutching in her hand. "Neil, look at this. It's an e-mail about Brutus – I printed it out."

"From his owner?" Neil asked, grabbing at the paper.

"No, from somebody who knows him. Read it."

Neil looked at the e-mail. It read:

I think Brutus is the dog who used to live next door to us. His owner

31

*has gone away. If you ring me I'll
tell you all about him.*

There was a Padsham phone number, and the name Jackie Meadows.

"I'm going to ring right now," Neil said.

"Don't be long, then," said Carole. "I'm just about to dish up lunch."

"Five minutes, Mum – OK?" When his mum nodded, Neil went out to the phone in the hall and Emily followed him. He rang the number printed at the bottom of the e-mail. The phone was answered almost at once.

A woman's voice said, "Yes?"

"Hello," Neil said. "Is that Jackie Meadows?"

"No, it's her mother. Who's calling, please?"

"I'm Neil Parker, from King Street Kennels in Compton." Neil explained about the e-mail from Jackie. "Could I speak to her, please?"

"I'll go and fetch her," the woman said. "Please hold on."

Neil waited, fizzing with impatience.

"What did they say?" Emily asked. "What's going on?"

"She's fetching Jackie," Neil told her, as a voice at the other end of the phone said, "Hello, this is Jackie Meadows."

"Hi," said Neil. "I'm Neil Parker from King

Street Kennels. You sent us an e-mail about Brutus."

"That's right," Jackie said. Neil thought she sounded friendly. "I often have a look at your site. I really love dogs."

"You said you know all about Brutus," Neil prompted, barely able to contain his eagerness. It looked like they were about to solve the mystery of Brutus's past.

"I'm sure it's the same dog," Jackie told him. "His owner used to live next door to us, but he went away a couple of weeks ago – he got a new job in Manchester. The house is empty now."

"That would explain why I couldn't get through on the phone," Neil said.

"I thought he must have taken Brutus with him," Jackie went on. "There's been no sign of him round here. I was really surprised when I saw his picture on your website."

"We found him hiding behind the bins at our school," Neil said. "He was starving, and he looks really thin."

"Oh, no!" The voice at the other end of the phone sounded indignant. "And he's such a lovely dog. He doesn't deserve that."

"So, what—" Neil was interrupted by Emily grabbing his arm.

33

"What does she say? Does she know our Brutus?" she demanded.

At the same moment, Carole's voice came from the kitchen. "Lunch!"

"Look," Neil said to Jackie, "I can't talk properly now. Would it be OK to come round and see you?" He remembered that his mum had threatened to take them Christmas shopping in Padsham that afternoon. "Will you be in after lunch?"

"Yes, that's fine," Jackie said. "We live on Orchard Road in Padsham – number 12. It's just past the swimming pool."

"Right, I know where that is." Neil and Emily had often gone swimming in the Padsham pool. "We'll see you later, then."

He put the phone down and turned to Emily. "We're going round to see Jackie this afternoon," he announced.

Emily's face split into a grin. "Great."

"She sounds really nice," Neil added, as they headed for the kitchen. "And she said Brutus is a lovely dog. That doesn't sound as if he is usually savage."

"Yes," Emily said thoughtfully. "So maybe this afternoon we'll find out what happened to change him."

Chapter Four

That afternoon, Carole drove Neil, Emily and Sarah into Padsham in the King Street Kennels Range Rover. They arranged to meet a couple of hours later, which would give Neil and Emily enough time to visit Jackie Meadows and finish off the last of their Christmas shopping.

The centre of Padsham was bright with Christmas lights. The sound of carols came from loudspeakers on a stall where the local Rotary club was collecting for children's charities. All the shop windows were hung with glittery decorations and sprayed with fake snow.

Neil and Emily headed out of the town centre

past the swimming pool. Though the snow had stopped falling, an icy wind swept down the road towards them, stinging their faces. Neil kept his head down and pulled up the hood of his jacket. Beside him, Jake trotted along the slushy pavement as if he didn't mind the cold at all.

"I wish I was a dog!" Neil muttered. "I'd have a built-in fur coat!"

Number 12, Orchard Road turned out to be a modern red-brick house. The snow in the front garden was well-trodden and a lopsided snowman stood in the middle. A Christmas tree with flashing lights stood inside the front window.

Next to it, number 14 was dark and quiet. There were no curtains at the windows, and the snow in the garden was undisturbed. An estate agent's board, which read TO LET, stood beside the gate.

"That must be where Brutus lived," said Emily.

Neil pushed open the gate of number 12 and led the way up the path. Almost as soon as he pressed the bell the door was opened, as if someone had been looking out for them.

In the doorway stood a girl of about his own

age. She was shorter than Neil, with frizzy brown hair in bunches. She wore jeans and a red sweatshirt with a reindeer on the front.

"Hi," she said, smiling brightly. "You must be Neil Parker. I'm Jackie. Come in."

Neil stepped into the hall, glad to be out of the cold wind. "Yes, I'm Neil. This is my sister Emily – and Jake."

Jackie said hello to Emily and bent down to talk to Jake. Neil noticed that she didn't make any sudden movements and that she held out her hand for Jake to sniff before she tried to pat him. Neil could see that Jackie was someone who really understood dogs.

"Have you got a dog of your own?" he asked.

Jackie shook her head regretfully. "I'd love one, but—" She broke off as a door opened behind her and a woman came out into the hall.

Neil guessed that she must be Jackie's mum; she looked exactly like an older version of Jackie, except that her frizzy hair was cut short. A small boy with fair hair was peering curiously round her legs.

"You must be the Parkers," said Mrs Meadows warmly. "Jackie, why don't you take them into the front room? Would you like some hot chocolate?"

"Yes, please!" Neil and Emily said together.

The woman vanished again and Jackie opened the door beside her and showed Neil and Emily into the cosy room. Another small boy, identical to the first, was sitting in the middle of the carpet in a nest of Christmas wrapping paper, winding ribbon round himself.

"No, Ben!" Jackie swooped on him and started to unwind the ribbon. Laughing, she added, "That's to wrap parcels with, not you! Or shall I wrap you up and send you through the post?"

"Post," the little boy agreed, with a big grin.

Jackie untangled the last of the ribbon and

steered Ben towards the door. "Go into the kitchen and play with Nicky. Mum might have something for you."

"Bikkit," Ben said hopefully and trotted out.

Still smiling, Jackie sank into a chair, and started to wind the ribbon up. "Little brothers! I love them to bits, but they drive me crazy. And that's why we don't have a dog. Mum and Dad think it wouldn't be safe until the twins are a bit older."

"We've always had dogs," Neil said.

"And we've got a little sister too," Emily added.

Jackie shrugged. "You'll have a job to persuade Mum."

We might try that, Neil thought as he took off his jacket and sat down. It looked like Jackie was part of a big, friendly family. And, in Neil's opinion, a family wasn't complete without a dog. "OK," he said. "Tell us about Brutus."

"Well . . ." Jackie leant forward, starting to look more serious. "Our next door neighbour was a guy called Simon Soames. He worked nights as an engineer on the local radio station. Last year his girlfriend gave him Brutus as a Christmas present."

"Uh-oh!" Neil rolled his eyes. "I can guess

what you're going to say. This Simon Soames had no idea his girlfriend was going to give him a puppy, right?"

"Right," said Jackie. She sounded angry. "It was a big surprise."

Emily let out a snort of indignation. "People are so stupid! Owning a dog is a *huge* responsibility. You should never give one as a present without making sure the owner knows what they're taking on."

"Too right!" Jackie agreed. "Anyway, at first I thought it would be OK. Brutus was a cute little pup and Simon and his girlfriend – Marilyn – spent ages playing with him in the garden. The problems started when Brutus got bigger."

Before Jackie could tell them what the problems were, the door opened and Mrs Meadows came into the room with a tray. It held mugs of hot chocolate, a plate of mince pies, and another of chocolate biscuits.

"Great!" said Neil. "Thanks, Mrs Meadows."

"It's a pleasure," said Mrs Meadows, setting the tray down on the coffee table in front of the fire. "Especially if you can do something to help Brutus. I've been really worried about that dog."

Just then a crash sounded from somewhere along the hall. "Nicky! Ben!" Mrs Meadows

40

called and hurried out.

Jackie handed round the mugs of chocolate. Jake got up from the hearthrug and came to look interestedly at the plates.

"Can I give him a biscuit?" Jackie asked.

Neil started to fish out his dog treats and then put them away again. "Just one," he said. "After all, it *is* Christmas."

Jake crunched the chocolate biscuit enthusiastically, but he was well-trained enough to realize that there wouldn't be any more. He made himself comfortable on the rug again.

"He's great," Jackie said admiringly. "Oh, I do wish we had a dog! Mum and Dad say when the boys go to school we can get one, but that's years away."

"Go on about Brutus," Neil prompted her.

"Right, where was I? Oh, yes, when Brutus got bigger . . . Well, Simon didn't have a lot of free time to give to Brutus. He slept during the day and worked at night and in his spare time he went out with Marilyn. He seemed to think that it was enough just to feed Brutus and leave him in the garden."

"All by himself?" exclaimed Emily. "That's *awful*! Dobermans need to be around people

41

and other dogs. I've been reading about them in my dog magazines. They aren't happy if they're left alone."

"I used to talk to him over the fence," said Jackie. "And after a bit I asked Simon if I could take him for walks. He said I could, because Brutus's barking disturbed him when he was trying to sleep. Simon couldn't see that the barking was *his* fault."

"He sounds a real idiot," said Neil.

"Well, ignorant about dogs," said Jackie. "Anyway, I used to walk Brutus most days after school. He had a basket and his lead in the garden shed, so I just used to collect him whenever I could. I—"

"You mean he wasn't allowed into the house?" Emily interrupted, her eyes wide with shock.

Jackie shook her head. "I reckon Simon was doing his best to forget that he ever had a dog. Which meant that, apart from me, Brutus hardly saw anybody. When I went over there he used to get so excited, he'd bark his head off and start jumping up. I taught him to sit, but he wouldn't do it for Simon. Simon would just yell at Brutus, and that didn't do any good at all."

Neil nodded. "Dogs don't understand if you shout. They get upset."

"The barking got so bad that the neighbours started to complain," Jackie went on. "So Simon bought this really tight muzzle and made Brutus wear it."

Neil and Emily exchanged a glance. "So *that's* why Brutus always growls at Dad!" said Emily.

Neil explained to Jackie how Bob had muzzled Brutus while they got him safely to the rescue centre and how Brutus was more mistrustful of Bob than anyone else.

"You can't blame him," Jackie said. "And the muzzle wasn't the worst thing, either." She hesitated, took a gulp of her hot chocolate and went on. "I noticed a couple of times that Brutus looked a bit battered and once he was bleeding from his ear. I asked Simon what had happened and he said he'd got into a fight with another dog." She made a disbelieving noise. "I'd just like to know when Brutus ever had a chance to fight with other dogs. It wasn't when he was with me, that's for sure."

"You're saying *Simon* hurt him?" Neil asked. He couldn't remember ever feeling so disgusted. No wonder poor Brutus was nervous and aggressive.

Jackie shrugged. "If you can think of a better explanation, tell me what it is." She handed round the last of the mince pies and the three of them sat munching.

Neil thought over what he had heard. His first determination to find Brutus's owner had changed into a fierce resolve not to give the Doberman back to Simon Soames, whatever happened. Not that it sounded as if Simon would *want* him back. "So what happened when Simon left?" he asked.

"Let me show you something," Jackie said. She stood up, brushing pastry crumbs off her sweatshirt. "Put your coats on, it's in the back garden."

Neil and Emily picked up their jackets and followed Jackie along the hall into the kitchen, with Jake trotting at their heels. Ben and Nicky were squidging plasticine at the kitchen table, while Mrs Meadows stirred something in a pan on the cooker.

"We're just going out for a minute, Mum," Jackie said, taking a thick padded jacket from a peg by the back door.

Mrs Meadows nodded and smiled.

Jackie led the way into the snow-covered garden, to the fence which separated it from number 14. She pointed to the fence at the bottom of number 14's garden. "Do you see that?"

The daylight was fading, but Neil could just make out that one of the planks in the fence was hanging loose, with a space at the bottom big enough for a determined dog to wriggle through.

"Brutus ran away!" said Emily.

"Can't say I blame him," Neil added.

"He did it once before, about a month ago," Jackie explained. "I think he was so bored in the garden that he pulled the plank out himself and went out into the lane. That time he ended up in a garden further down the road and the people there brought him back. They were furious – he'd dug up some of their precious plants!"

"I bet Simon wasn't pleased," Neil said grimly, dreading to think how Soames might have punished the frustrated dog.

"You can say that again. But he didn't mend the fence. I reckon he was hoping that one day Brutus would wander off and not come back."

"But that's stupid!" Neil exploded. "If he didn't want Brutus, he could have found him another home. He could have brought him to us at King Street. We would have looked after him."

"Simon couldn't have cared less," said Jackie. She shivered. "It's freezing out here. Let's go back inside."

They crunched their way across the snowy patio and back into the kitchen. Mrs Meadows turned away from her cooking as they came in. "I can't tell you how pleased I am that someone is helping that poor dog," she said. "It's been worrying me for months. Even when I thought he'd gone off to Manchester with Simon, I couldn't get him out of my head."

"Did Simon even try to take Brutus with him?" Neil asked.

"I don't know," said Jackie. "Simon got a better job in Manchester, so he moved there a couple of weeks ago. Brutus disappeared about the same time, so I assumed Simon had taken him."

"Well, he never said he wasn't going to," said Mrs Meadows, taking her pan off the heat and pouring its contents into a pastry case. "Simon definitely told me he'd found a flat and—"

"But you can't keep a Doberman in a flat!" Emily was outraged. "They're big dogs. They need space."

"I bet Brutus didn't run away again," said Neil. "I bet Simon just left him behind."

"Well, I'm sorry to say it, but I wouldn't be at all surprised," said Mrs Meadows. "I just hope that now you'll be able to find him a really good home with people who care about him."

"We'll certainly try," said Neil.

"I'll give you Simon's new address and phone number," Mrs Meadows said, wiping her hands on a towel and picking up a pad and pencil from the kitchen dresser. "I suppose you'll have to check that he really doesn't want Brutus."

As she scribbled down the details, an idea

began to grow in Neil's mind. Trying to sound casual, he said, "Would you like to come over and visit Brutus? I bet he'd like to see some old friends."

"Can we, Mum?" Jackie said, beaming. "I've really missed him."

"Well, I don't see why not." Mrs Meadows smiled as she gave Neil the piece of paper with Simon Soames's address on it. "You'd like to go and see Brutus, wouldn't you?" she asked the twins.

"Big dog," said Ben solemnly.

"That's right," Emily said. "We've got lots of dogs for you to see."

Ben's twin, Nicky, started bouncing up and down and banging the table with a wooden spoon. "See lots of dogs!" he agreed.

Neil exchanged a sympathetic glance with Jackie. Ben and Nicky were even more noisy than his little sister Sarah! "Come any time," he said. "Best to give us a ring first, though."

He and Emily said goodbye to the Meadows and set off back to the town centre. There was just time to finish their Christmas shopping before they had to meet their mum.

"That was a good idea," said Emily. "Inviting them to come and visit. I really like them. And I bet it'll help Brutus to see his friends again."

"That's not all." Neil grinned. "Brutus can't go back to Simon, right?"

"Right!" Emily agreed firmly.

"So he needs a good home. Well, I reckon I've just found one," said Neil confidently.

Emily paused, her mouth open with surprise. "The Meadows? But you heard what Jackie said. Their mum and dad won't let them have a dog until the boys are bigger."

"Then we'll just have to hope they change their mind – won't we, boy?" Neil said to Jake.

Jake let out an approving bark.

"Jackie and her family are the perfect owners for Brutus," Neil went on. "They just don't know it yet!"

Chapter Five

When the Parkers arrived back at King Street Kennels, another car was already parked there.

"Mike's here!" Neil exclaimed.

He and Emily piled out of the Range Rover, up the steps to the front door and into the house. Through the open door of the utility room Neil could hear voices – his dad's and the vet's.

"I've no worries about Willow at all, physically," Mike Turner was saying. "She's a healthy dog and she's in great shape to have her pups."

"That's good to hear," said Bob.

Neil went into the utility room with Emily behind him. Mike was squatting on the floor beside Willow, who was lying on her side in the whelping box. He grinned up at Neil and Emily as they came in and beckoned them across. "Here," he said to Neil, holding out a stethoscope. "Come and listen to this."

Neil fitted the hooks into his ears and Mike held the end to Willow's stomach. Neil could hear a very faint, rhythmic sound. "What is it?" he asked.

"Willow's pups," said Mike with a grin. "That's their heartbeat."

"Wow!" said Neil. He could hardly believe he was actually listening to the tiny, living creatures inside Willow.

The little white dog turned her head to see what he was doing and then turned away again. Neil thought she still looked listless, not the bright, happy dog she usually was.

He passed the stethoscope to Emily so that she could have a turn and watched an incredulous smile spread across her face as she listened to the muffled sounds. "That's so cool!" she breathed.

"As I said, Bob," Mike went on, "I've no real worries about Willow's health, but she does seem a bit depressed."

"I think she's missing Kate and Glen," Emily said, handing the stethoscope back to Mike. "Let's invite them round for supper – we can, can't we, Mum?" Emily twisted round to look at Carole, who had just appeared in the doorway of the utility room.

Carole agreed that was a great idea and Emily went off to phone Kate and Glen.

Mike Turner gave Willow a farewell pat and started to pack up his equipment. "See she gets plenty to eat," he said to Neil, "but don't let her stuff herself. If she overeats, she'll have more trouble delivering her pups. And gentle exercise is good. She'll know how much she feels like doing."

"Right!" said Neil. "You can rely on the Puppy Patrol!" He bent down to ruffle Willow's wiry coat. "Don't worry, girl. It won't be long now."

"How did you get on this afternoon?" Bob asked Neil as they went back into the kitchen.

Neil launched into the story of how Brutus had been mistreated by his previous owner. By the time he had finished, Bob was frowning thoughtfully.

"That certainly explains a lot," he said. "It's tough for Brutus – his temperament could be permanently spoilt by a bad start like that."

"I don't believe it!" Emily said hotly. "Brutus is great – he just needs proper care, that's all."

Bob smiled. "You might be right. We'll do what we can, at any rate."

"Would you like me to take a look at him?" Mike Turner offered.

"Yes, please," Bob replied. "I'm pretty sure there's nothing wrong with him, though, apart from lack of food while he was living rough."

"A check-up will do no harm," said Mike. "And if you want to take this further, it might be helpful to have my opinion of the dog's condition."

Bob scratched his beard. "That's true."

"Do you think we should do something about

53

Simon Soames?" Neil asked. "Mrs Meadows gave me his new address and phone number. Do you want to ring him?"

"I don't think so," said Bob. "The person I want to ring is Terri McCall. I think the RSPCA should know what's going on." He glanced at his watch. "I should just be able to catch her. Neil, you take Mike out to see Brutus."

Neil fished in his pocket for the piece of paper Mrs Meadows had given him and handed it to his dad. Then he led Mike out to the rescue centre.

Snow started to fall again as they crossed the courtyard, but inside the rescue centre it was invitingly warm. Brutus was lying down when Neil and Mike went in, but he leapt to his feet as they approached the pen and retreated to the back wall.

"He's a fine-looking chap," Mike observed. "Let's take a closer look, shall we?"

Neil opened the door of the pen. He knew his dad wouldn't mind him going in when Mike was with him.

Brutus didn't growl or show any other signs of aggression, but Neil could see he was trembling. He fished in his pocket for a dog treat and dropped it on the floor by his boots.

After a short hesitation, Brutus came up to him and took it.

"He's starting to trust you, at least," said Mike. "Can you hold him for me while I examine him? We'll muzzle him first if you like."

"Oh, no," Neil said. "Nobody's going to put a muzzle on Brutus again – are they, boy?" He crouched down beside the Doberman and put a hand on his flank. He could feel how tense the dog was. "Take it easy, boy," he said soothingly. "Mike's just going to take a look at you."

Neil kept one hand on Brutus's collar and talked to him as the vet gave him a thorough examination. As he stroked the sleek black-and-tan coat, Neil could feel Brutus starting to relax.

"Well," Mike said at last, sitting back on his heels, "I don't think I can tell you anything you don't know already. There's nothing serious wrong with him. He's been pretty hungry for a while, but he's getting over that. There are one or two small scars – here, look, and here." He gently tilted Brutus's head towards the light. "I doubt they're dog bites. My guess would be that someone hit him with something thin, like a stick."

Neil felt sick. "I'd like to hit Simon Soames with a stick!"

"The RSPCA will take care of Soames, I reckon," said Mike. "Hitting any dog is a foul thing to do, but Dobermans in particular can't stand it. It confuses them and makes them angry." He gave Brutus a pat. "Never mind, boy. You're in good hands now."

Neil took out another dog treat and dropped it on the floor in front of Brutus. The Doberman crunched it and gave Neil a bright, alert look, as if he wanted more. Neil suddenly felt hopeful. He'd never seen Brutus look quite so friendly before.

He took out another titbit and, daringly, held it out on the palm of his hand. Brutus nuzzled him, his lips feeling soft and velvety, and took the treat gently.

Neil patted him. "That's right, boy. You know you're OK now, don't you?"

Brutus flopped down on the ground again, his head raised and alert. He already looked like a different dog from the one Neil and Emily had found poking around the school bins.

"If he goes on like this, you won't have any trouble re-homing him," said Mike.

Neil grinned. "I know! And I've got just the people in mind!"

*

When Kate and Glen arrived for supper, Neil could see how tired Kate was looking. She was moving very slowly and awkwardly – just like Willow, who came padding out to greet her.

"I'm really missing her," Kate confessed, reaching down to ruffle Willow's ears. "But I know she's in the right place here. I couldn't even bend down to put her food on the floor!"

While they ate, Neil told Kate and Glen about Brutus and what he had heard about the Doberman's previous owner.

"People like that shouldn't be allowed to keep a dog," said Glen, who was involved with a local animal rights group. "Brutus will be lucky if he's not damaged permanently."

"He's a great dog!" Neil insisted. "He's going to be fine."

When the meal was over, Kate made herself comfortable on the sofa in the sitting-room, with Willow tucked next to her. She stroked the little dog's fur lovingly.

"Why don't you go and see this new dog?" she suggested to Glen. "Willow and I will just enjoy each other's company for a bit."

Neil and Glen went out to the rescue centre. Brutus raised his head as they went up to the pen, but for the first time he had enough confidence not to retreat to the back wall.

Neil could see the admiration in Glen's eyes as he studied the powerful Doberman. Brutus's black-and-tan coat gleamed and his eyes shone with intelligence as he looked steadily back at them.

"Hi there, boy," Glen said, slipping a dog treat through the mesh. "It beats me how anyone could ill-treat a fantastic dog like that," he added.

Neil shrugged. He'd given up trying to understand people like Simon Soames.

"Well, Brutus," said Glen. The young Doberman pricked his ears as if he was listening.

"You've got nothing to worry about now. You've got the Puppy Patrol to look after you!"

When Neil and Glen went back to the house, they found Kate and Willow peacefully asleep in front of the fire.

Glen shook his wife's shoulder gently to wake her. "Come on, love, it's time to go home."

Kate blinked and yawned and ran her hand sadly over Willow's head. "I really hate leaving her."

"Not long now," Glen said comfortingly, patting Kate's enormous tummy. "I'm just waiting to see who's going to win this race!"

The next day was Christmas Eve. Neil and Emily were putting the finishing touches to the tree in the sitting-room when the phone rang. A moment later, Neil heard his mum's voice. "Neil, it's for you."

"Hi, it's Jackie," said a cheerful voice as he picked the phone up. "Listen, Mum and Dad want to come over to Compton to see Gran, and we thought we could drop into King Street – if that's OK with you."

"That's fine," said Neil. "Come as soon as you like." He went back into the sitting-room to tell Emily the news.

His sister had just draped the last piece of tinsel over the tree and was standing back to admire the effect. "Great," she said, when Neil told her his news. "Are you going to ask them if they'll take Brutus?"

"I'm not sure," Neil said. "I don't want to rush them, but they might not come here again. I think I'll just play it by ear."

He still wasn't sure when Jackie arrived with her mum and a tall, dark-haired man who introduced himself as Jackie's father, Alan.

"We left Nicky and Ben with Gran," Jackie explained.

"I'm sure the dogs wouldn't scare them," Emily said.

Jackie giggled. "No, but they might scare the dogs!"

Neil showed Mr and Mrs Meadows into the office to say hello to Carole, who was working on the computer, and then he and Emily took them to see Brutus.

"What a fantastic place!" Jackie exclaimed as Neil led the way into the rescue centre. "And there's Brutus – hi there, boy! Do you remember me?"

She hardly needed to ask. Brutus had been lying in his pen, dozing, but as soon as he heard

the sound of her voice he leapt to his feet and
let out a joyous bark. A second later, to Neil's
amazement, the dog reared up against the
mesh, his paws splayed out, panting eagerly as
Jackie came towards him.

Neil couldn't believe the change in Brutus.
This was the first time he had ever come up to
the mesh by himself, without someone coaxing
him. For a nervous and unhappy dog, he
suddenly seemed eager and friendly.

That settles it, Neil said to himself. *Jackie* has
to be the right owner for Brutus.

Jackie went up to Brutus, a delighted smile

on her face, and reached out to rub his nose through the mesh. "He looks fine," she said to Neil.

"You should have seen him a couple of days ago," Neil said. "He was really thin and you could see all his ribs. But we've been feeding him up. Mike Turner, the vet, says there's nothing wrong with him."

"I'm so relieved!" said Mrs Meadows. "Before you came to see us, I hadn't been able to get the poor creature out of my mind. Even when I thought he was with Simon, I was worried that he wouldn't be properly looked after."

"Horrible man!" said Jackie. "Never mind," she added to Brutus. "You won't have to go back to him ever again!"

Neil handed Jackie a dog treat and she offered it to Brutus through the mesh. The young Doberman took it gently and his tail started to wag. Neil stared. In all Brutus's time at King Street, he had never wagged his tail before.

"So what happens now?" Mr Meadows asked. "Will you be able to find him a new home?"

"Oh, yes," said Emily confidently. "His details are on our website and after Christmas I'm going to ask Jake Fielding if he'll put something in the *Compton News*. We're sure to find someone who wants him."

Neil looked at Brutus, who was sniffing happily at Jackie's hands. "He can stay here until we find the right owners for him," he said. *And with any luck*, he added silently, *that won't be very long*. He paused, while Jackie went on petting Brutus, and then thought, *Go for it!*

"Of course," Neil went on, "the people who take him will have to understand what he went through. He'll need a lot of care and love. I think you could do a great job, if you wanted to. He already loves Jackie – you can see he does."

Jackie spun round, her face alight. "Mum, Dad – can we?"

Mr and Mrs Meadows exchanged a thoughtful look and for a minute Neil thought they were going to say yes.

Then Mrs Meadows slowly shook her head. "I'm sorry. If it was just the three of us . . . but I can't be sure that Brutus would be safe with the twins. They're too little to understand about being careful with him."

"I'd look after him, Mum," Jackie said.

"And we'll stay in touch," Emily added. "We'll give you all the help we can."

"That's not the point," Jackie's dad said. "The

point is that Brutus has had a really bad start in life and I don't think we're the right people to take him on."

"But—" Neil began.

"No, Neil," Mr Meadows interrupted. He sounded genuinely sorry. "We're all fond of Brutus, but our children's safety has to come first. It's too much of a risk." He touched his wife's sleeve, indicating that they should leave.

All the happiness had drained out of Jackie's face. There were tears in her eyes as she rubbed Brutus's head for one last time. "Goodbye, boy," she whispered. Then she turned away and walked out of the rescue centre with her head down.

Her parents followed.

Mrs Meadows paused to say, "We're really sorry." She squeezed Neil's arm and smiled at him.

Emily went with them to show them out, but Neil stayed with Brutus. Once Jackie had gone, the young dog lay down again. He looked sad too. He put his nose on his paws and kept his eyes fixed on the door as if he was waiting for Jackie to come back.

He perked up when the door opened again, but it was only Emily. She was shaking her head. "They're such nice people," she said.

"I know," said Neil. "I just can't understand why they won't see that Brutus is the dog for them."

Emily shrugged. "They're worried about their children."

"But Brutus isn't dangerous!" Neil protested. "I know he isn't. But Jackie's parents just won't believe it. And you know what?" he added. "We'll have the same problem with anyone else who comes to look at Brutus. We'll *have* to tell them all about his past. And then they'll expect him to be dangerous as well." Neil stared gloomily through the mesh at the homeless dog. "It's not going to be as easy as we thought. Maybe no one at all will want him."

Chapter Six

"**T**here!" Carole Parker said, as she put the last gift-wrapped present under the tree. "All ready for tomorrow." She started ticking items off on her fingers. "I've stuffed the turkey, I've made another batch of mince pies – where did the last ones go, Neil? – I've iced the cake . . ."

"I went out and cut the holly," Neil said in an injured tone. Emily had eaten just as many mince pies as he had. "And washed up after lunch."

"*We* washed up after lunch," Emily reminded him. "I'm sure everything's ready, Mum."

"It had better be." Carole glanced at her watch. "Let's see if your dad's got supper ready.

And don't forget you've got to stay awake for Midnight Mass!"

As they trooped into the kitchen, the phone rang. Neil picked it up. "King Street Kennels. Can I help you?"

"Hi, Neil." It was Terri McCall, the local RSPCA officer.

"Hi!" Neil said eagerly. "Have you done any more about Brutus's owner?"

"I certainly have," Terri said. "I gave the Manchester RSPCA office all the details, along with Simon Soames's new address, and they decided to hand everything over to the local police." Her voice grew serious. "Mr Soames will be getting a visitor soon and it won't be Father Christmas."

"That's great news," said Neil. "I'll tell Dad."

"Thanks – and thanks for your help, Neil."

"It's a pleasure," said Neil. "Happy Christmas!"

"Happy Christmas!" said Terri, and rang off.

The bells of Compton Parish Church were ringing as Bob Parker steered the Range Rover into the church car park. All the Parkers were muffled up in coats and scarves, and Sarah was bouncing up and down in excitement because, for the first time ever, she was being allowed to stay up for Midnight Mass. She had insisted on wearing her sparkly angel costume from the infants' Nativity Play; Neil hoped no one would notice it under her thick coat. Little sisters could be *so* embarrassing!

The night was clear and cold. A million stars twinkled above them and thick snow glittered on the gravestones. The door to the church stood open, shedding warm yellow candlelight onto the path.

Neil thought it looked as if half of Compton was walking through the churchyard. Within a couple of minutes, he had said hello to Sergeant Moorhead, Mr Hamley and his wife Rachel, and Dr Harvey, who was with an elderly lady who, Neil guessed, was his mother.

Further away, Neil spotted his classmate Hasheem Lindon with his sister Rehana and their parents, while Emily darted off to wish a Happy Christmas to her best friend Julie Baker. Neil was just waving to Mrs Smedley from the newsagent's when he heard a voice behind him.

"Happy Christmas, all of you!"

It was Mike Turner.

"Happy Christmas, Mike!" Neil said.

"I'll be on call over Christmas," Mike said as they reached the church porch. "If you need any help with Willow, just give me a ring on my mobile."

"Fine, we'll do that," Bob said. "I'm not expecting any trouble, but it's good to know you're available."

"You're not on your own over Christmas, are you?" Carole asked anxiously.

"No, I'm going to my sister's," Mike said. "Don't worry. She always cooks a stunning Christmas lunch!"

They went into the church. Emily gasped. "It's so beautiful!" she exclaimed, gazing around her.

Neil had to agree. Every corner of the church was lit by candles, in the pews, on the altar and in a row of chandeliers above the central aisle. At the far end was a huge Christmas tree, hung with silver foil stars, and near the entrance was a Christmas crib.

The organ started to play as the Parkers squashed into a pew. Neil got ready to have a good sing. Even if he did have a voice like a dog with kennel cough, nobody minded at Christmas!

The vicar, Gavin Thorpe, was standing beside

the pulpit, beaming at everyone. Neil was used to seeing him with his black Labrador, Jet, at his heels. He thought it was a pity that Jet couldn't be with Gavin now. Neil would have liked to bring Jake, although he had to admit that Midnight Mass would probably be a bit too crowded if everyone brought their pets along as well.

But when the service was over and the Parkers were lining up with everyone else to shake hands with Gavin on the way out, Neil saw that Jet had appeared from somewhere and was sitting beside his owner.

As soon as he was close enough, Neil fished out a dog treat and bent down to give it to Jet. The Labrador looked alert and happy and he had a Christmas bauble tied to his collar.

"Hi there, Jet," said Neil. "Where did you spring from?"

"He's been waiting for me in the vestry," Gavin explained. "I thought he might be lonely, all by himself in the vicarage."

"He behaved very well," Carole said. "No one would have known he was there."

"You're a great dog, Jet," Neil said, rumpling the Labrador's ears. "And you're to have a great Christmas, do you hear?"

Jet thumped his tail on the flagstones as if in agreement and gave Neil's hand a lick. Neil stroked his smooth head once more and hurried after his mum and dad.

By the time the Parkers got back to King Street, Sarah was yawning and hardly able to keep her eyes open. Carole took her inside to bed, while Bob, Neil and Emily did a final check of the kennel blocks and the rescue centre.

Neil offered to take a look at Brutus, who was all on his own now that the other two rescue dogs had been collected by their new families.

As Neil came in, Brutus raised his head, gave Neil a drowsy look and settled down again.

"Merry Christmas, Brutus," Neil said softly. "And a Happy New Year – I'll make sure of that."

He was letting himself out of the rescue centre again when he heard a loud barking coming from the house. "That's Jake!" he exclaimed.

Neil dashed across the courtyard and through the back door. The barking continued. The kitchen was in darkness. Neil switched on the light and saw Jake standing in the doorway to the utility room and barking his head off.

"Jake!" Neil exclaimed. "What is it, boy?" He crouched down to pat the Border collie. Jake stopped barking and whined softly. Neil looked past him into the utility room, where Willow lay in the whelping box.

One look was enough.

Neil dashed out again and almost collided with Bob, who was returning from Kennel Block One.

"Dad!" Neil gasped. "Come quick! It's Willow – she's having her pups!"

Chapter Seven

"**S**teady on," said Bob. "No need to panic. Let's go and take a look."

He went indoors, and Neil followed him, along with Emily, who had just appeared from Kennel Block Two. Jake settled down near the door of the utility room, his ears pricked as if he understood what was going on.

Neil paused to pat him. "Well done, boy. You warned us, didn't you?"

Willow was shifting restlessly in the whelping box. She was panting rapidly, and she kept turning to lick her hindquarters. As Neil watched, a strong muscular ripple passed over her body.

Bob bent down and checked her gently.

73

"She's well into second stage labour," he reported. "Emily, you'll find the things we need in that cupboard – could you get them out for me, please?"

Emily hurried across to fetch the towels and other equipment that Carole had got ready as soon as Willow arrived.

Meanwhile, Bob gave his hands a thorough wash. "You should find a hot water bottle in there as well," he said to Emily. "Fill it for me, please – not too hot – and wrap it in a blanket."

While Emily disappeared into the kitchen, Neil went over to Willow and crouched down to stroke the top of her head gently. Willow licked his hand. "You're doing just fine, girl," Neil told her. "Those pups will be here before you know it."

Another powerful ripple ran across Willow's swollen abdomen. Neil knew that meant the first pup was passing down the birth canal, getting ready to be born.

Neil had watched Delilah giving birth to Jake and the rest of the litter, and Mr Hamley's Dalmatian Dotty having her pups, so he knew what to expect, but he still felt so excited he could hardly breathe.

"Come on, girl, push," Neil encouraged

Willow. "You can do it!"

Emily came back into the utility room with the hot water bottle wrapped in a fleecy blanket and Bob tucked it into the whelping box beside Willow.

Emily crouched beside Neil. "Do you think she'll be all right?"

"No reason why not," Bob replied. "But with a first litter it's always good to be careful. Hello!" he said suddenly. "Here we go!"

Willow panted and pushed. A tiny shape appeared from her hindquarters, wrapped in what looked like a bag. Neil knew this was the birth sac which protected the puppy as it grew inside its mother.

"Willow, you've done it!" Emily breathed. "Your very first pup."

The newborn pup was still connected to Willow by the cord which had fed it inside her womb. As if someone had taught her what to do, Willow twisted round so she could reach the cord and bit through it. Then she licked the pup vigorously to get rid of the birth sac.

The pup let out a faint whimpering sound, as if it was protesting.

Bob was grinning. "It's a girl," he announced and added, "It must be a shock, coming out into the big, wide world. It's OK, little one. We'll look after you." He had a towel in his hand, ready to clean up the pup's eyes and mouth, but Willow was doing the job efficiently by herself.

After a minute or two the pup wriggled close to her mum, fastened onto one of her teats, and began to suck.

"Brilliant!" Neil said quietly. "Absolutely brilliant!"

Willow nosed the little pup affectionately, and Emily reached out to stroke her damp, white fur with one finger. "She's so tiny!" she said. "Dad, how many pups will Willow have? Dotty had eight!"

"Not as many as that," Bob said. "As a rough guide, the bigger the dog, the bigger the litter. Willow should—"

He broke off as Willow began to pant hard again and he lifted the first pup away from her mum and onto the hot water bottle. The puppy protested with a tiny squeak.

"Sorry, midget," Bob said. "I'll put you back in a minute. Willow might hurt her by mistake while the next one's coming out," he explained to Neil and Emily.

As he spoke, a second puppy appeared from Willow's hindquarters. Bob checked it quickly.

"This one's a boy," he said.

Willow cleaned him up like the first one and gently nudged him towards her teats. Bob replaced the first pup and soon the two little bundles of white fluff were sucking happily side by side.

Once the second puppy was feeding, Willow seemed to settle down for a rest. She dropped her nose onto her paws, closed her eyes, and let out a deep sigh.

"Do you think she's finished?" Neil asked. "After just two pups?"

"Maybe," said Bob. "But it's not unusual to

have a long gap between pups. I'll stay and keep an eye on her, but you two go to bed if you like."

"And miss some more pups being born?" Neil said. "No way!"

For a while it looked as if nothing else was happening. Emily went into the kitchen to make some hot chocolate and Carole came down from putting Sarah to bed.

Emily was handing round the hot drinks when Neil noticed that Willow had started to shift uncomfortably. "I think she's started again," he said.

Bob moved the two pups onto the hot water bottle to give Willow more room. For a long time Willow panted and strained, but the puppy didn't appear.

"What's the matter with her?" Neil asked anxiously.

"Probably nothing," Bob said reassuringly, though Neil noticed he was starting to look worried. "The birth can take longer as the mother gets more tired. Or it might mean that the pup is in an awkward position in the birth canal, so it's harder for the mother to push it out."

"Should we ring Mike?" Neil suggested.

"Not yet," said Bob. "Let's give Willow a bit longer first."

Emily crouched down beside Willow and stroked her head gently. "Kate will never forgive us if anything goes wrong," she said.

Neil thought Willow was starting to look exhausted. It was hard work, bringing puppies into the world.

Neil was just beginning to fidget, wanting to go and ring Mike Turner, when suddenly Emily exclaimed, "Look! The puppy's coming!"

Relief washed over Neil as he saw another tiny puppy starting to emerge.

"Breech birth," said Bob, sounding serious. "That means the legs are coming first instead of the head. No wonder it was stuck!"

"It's awfully small," Emily said.

Neil could see she was right. This pup was a lot smaller than the two that were now cuddled against the hot water bottle. He started to get anxious again, especially when the pup lay motionless as Willow bit through the cord and licked away the birth sac.

"Is it alive?" Emily asked, her voice tight.

"Can't tell yet," Bob said calmly. "Neil, hand me that towel."

Neil passed it over. Bob used it to pick up the

little pup, which lay limply in his hands. Very gently, he cleaned its eyes and mouth, and gave it a rub with the towel.

"It's dead!" Emily exclaimed.

"Ring Mike," said Bob, not taking his eyes off the pup.

Emily scrambled to her feet and went out to find Carole. Neil watched his dad, wishing there was something he could do. Willow let out a little whimper, as if she couldn't understand why this pup didn't behave like the others.

Bob climbed carefully to his feet. He held the tiny body between both hands and raised it high in the air.

Neil stared. He had no idea what his dad was doing.

Then Bob swung the pup vigorously towards the floor. "This can help clear fluid from the lungs," he explained.

The puppy didn't move. Bob tried the swing again and a third time.

Emily came back and watched wide-eyed, tears trickling down her face. "Mike's coming," she said. She was holding Carole's hand tightly.

Bob swung the pup a fourth time and at last Neil saw the tiny body twitch. "It's alive!" he said. He felt like jumping up and down and cheering, but he didn't want to startle Willow, who was watching Bob anxiously.

Bob used the towel to clear the pup's mouth again and gave it another gentle rub. It was wriggling feebly now and it let out a faint mewling noise.

"There we are," said Bob. "Another girl. Come on, little one, have a suck from your mum."

He put the third pup down in the whelping box, with her mouth near one of Willow's teats. But the puppy didn't start to feed; she just lay there. Willow tried to nudge her towards the teat but the tiny creature didn't respond.

"She's very weak," said Bob. "That long labour must have tired her out."

"But she'll die if she won't suck!" Emily cried.

"If she can't feed herself, we'll have to feed her," said Carole. "It'll be all right, Emily. It's not the first time. Remember those pups Toby Sparrow brought us? You managed brilliantly with them." She smiled encouragingly at Emily. "I think I've got some of the right milk formula," she added. "I'll go and look."

Bob put the other two pups back with their mum and they both started to suck. He tried again to get the third little pup to feed, but with no more success.

Neil kept his eyes fixed on the tiny scrap of white fluff as they waited for Mike Turner to come. It felt like an age. The pup didn't move again. Neil could see she was breathing, but he expected every feeble breath to be the last.

He realized he was digging his nails into the palms of his hands. *She won't die*! he vowed to himself.

"Come on," Bob said, trying to sound encouraging. "We've got three pups here. What are we going to call them?"

"Kate might not like our names," Emily pointed out, sniffing and scrubbing her eyes with the back of her hand.

"Then she can change them," said Bob. "The

pups will be too small to learn their names for a good while yet."

"Christmas names, then," said Emily, trying to smile. "Because they're born on Christmas morning. What do you think, Neil?"

"Sounds good to me," said Neil. "What about Angel?" He stroked the first pup very gently.

"With a name like that, she'd better be a *really* good dog!" Bob said, grinning.

"And this one can be Tinsel," Emily said, pointing to the second pup. "And the little one . . ."

Her voice faltered and Neil could tell she was thinking that the third pup might not need a name at all.

"The little one is Star," Neil said, speaking a bit louder than he'd meant to. "She's had a tough time, but she'll get over it. She'll be a real star!"

Emily managed a watery smile. "OK, Star it is!"

At last Neil heard the back door open and his mum reappeared, followed by Mike Turner. The vet put his bag down and knelt beside the whelping box. Bob explained to him what had happened.

Mike nodded, picked Star up and examined

her gently. "There's nothing obviously wrong," he said. "Sometimes you get a weak pup and the difficult birth wouldn't help." He paused and added, "Caring for her will be quite a job, you know."

"We can do it," Neil said determinedly. "Just tell us what she needs."

"Warmth is most important," Mike said. "Hypothermia is one of the commonest causes of death in new pups. This room feels fine and I see you've got the infra-red lamp, but you should check the temperature. It should be kept at 26 degrees."

"I'll fetch a thermometer," Carole said. "And we can bring in another heater if we need to."

"Fine," said Mike. "The next thing is, you need to keep an eye on Willow. Bitches have been known to reject their pups by pushing them out of the whelping box and letting them die."

"Willow wouldn't do that!" Emily exclaimed, sounding shocked.

"Even the best bitches have been known to harm their pups if they're disturbed after the birth. So it's important to keep Willow quiet and happy."

"No problem!" said Neil. He knew that Mike

was trying to make them realize how difficult it was going to be to look after Star, but there was no way Neil was going to let Willow's puppy down.

"And then there's feeding, of course," Mike went on. "The pup will need to be fed every two hours until she can suck from Willow herself. Once she can do that, you're home and dry."

"More broken nights!" Carole said.

"I can do it," Neil said. "I don't mind getting up."

"And me," said Emily.

"You'll need a special milk formula," Mike said. "I can go down to the surgery and fetch—"

"No need," Carole interrupted, showing him the packet she was carrying. "I always keep some of this on hand. It's useful if any of the young boarding dogs are off their food."

"That's fine," said Mike. "Have you got a small feeding bottle or a syringe?"

Carole nodded.

"I'm going to fetch some blankets," Neil said. "I'll make up a bed on the sitting-room sofa and then I'll be able to get up and feed Star."

"I want to do it as well," Emily said. "Mum, can we bring the folding bed down?"

"Yes, I'll help you," Carole said. "Just as soon as Mike has finished."

"Father Christmas won't come if you're not in bed and asleep," Bob said teasingly.

Neil laughed. In the drama of the last hour he'd forgotten all about Christmas presents. "I'm sure he'll time his visit for when we're not feeding Star," he said.

Neil woke in the dark with the loud ring of his alarm clock in his ear. For a second he couldn't think where he was. The room was dark, so it wasn't morning and he felt too tired to have slept through the night.

Then he remembered. He had promised to get up every two hours and feed Star. Before Mike Turner left, he had examined the other two pups and Willow herself. Thankfully they were all healthy and Willow hadn't got any more pups to come.

Neil pushed back his blankets and sat up. He was on the sitting-room sofa, and as his eyes got used to the faint light filtering in from the hall he could see Emily curled up on the folding bed beside him. The heavy weight across his feet was Jake.

Yawning, Neil crawled out of his blankets

and gave Emily a shake. Then he padded into the kitchen with Jake at his heels.

Carole had left the milk formula on the kitchen table, along with a measuring jug and a tiny feeding bottle. Mike Turner had written down the amount Star was to have and Carole had given her the first feed before he left. Neil and Emily had watched carefully so they knew what to do.

As Neil switched on the kettle and started to measure out the formula, Emily came in and went straight through to the utility room to check on Willow and the pups.

"They're fine," she told Neil. "Star's still alive."

Until then, Neil hadn't admitted to himself that she might not be. He didn't let Emily see how relieved he felt. "She's going to stay that way," he said firmly.

When the formula was ready, he took the feeding bottle into the utility room. Starlight was shining softly through the window. Willow and her pups were curled up together in the whelping box, all asleep. Bob and Carole had cleaned them up and given them fresh bedding when the birth was over.

"They're so sweet!" Emily murmured.

Carefully Neil picked Star out of the huddle of

puppies and cradled her on his lap. She was so tiny – a ball of white fluff small enough to nest in his hand, her eyes still tightly closed. Her fur was damp and frizzy where Willow had been cleaning her. She whimpered softly. Emily held the feeding bottle against Star's tiny lips, but at first she turned her head away.

"Remember what Mum did?" Neil said.

Emily nodded, and squeezed out a few drops of milk onto her fingers. She held them for Star to sniff and the pup put out a tiny pink tongue and licked at the milk. Emily offered her the bottle again and this time Star began to suck.

Neil felt a huge smile spreading over his face. "Magic!"

The whole house was quiet. Neil felt sleepy, but he wouldn't have missed this for the world. He gazed down at the little white bundle on his lap, and willed Star to keep drinking and make herself strong and healthy.

Star didn't finish the whole of the bottle before her head dropped and she went back to sleep. Emily took her from Neil, cuddled her for a moment and then put her carefully back into the whelping box with her mum.

Quietly Neil and Emily went back to the sitting-room. Neil set the alarm clock again; there would be one more feed before the rest of the house got up.

"Star's going to be OK!" Emily said with a blissful smile on her face as she climbed back into bed.

"Maybe," said Neil. He still couldn't help feeling worried. "Somehow, we've got to get her feeding from her mum." He frowned into the darkness. Little Star was clearly a fighter, but would that be enough?

Chapter Eight

Neil woke to the sound of footsteps going along the hall and a door opening and closing. Beside him on the folding bed, Emily rolled over and sat up.

They had woken up once more in the night to give Star another feed. Now Neil didn't know what time it was, but his stomach told him that breakfast was long overdue. A bulging Christmas stocking lay on the sofa at his feet, and there was another beside Emily's bed. "Hey!" he said. "Father Christmas came after all!"

Before he opened his presents, Neil wanted to check on Star. In the hall, Bob was putting the phone down. He had a wide grin on his face.

"Merry Christmas, Dad!" Neil said.

"Merry Christmas, Neil. I've just been talking to Glen."

"Did you tell him about the puppies?" Emily asked, emerging from the sitting-room. She was yawning and rubbing sleep out of her eyes.

Bob's eyes twinkled. "Let's go and find your mum first," he said, leading the way to the kitchen.

As Neil opened the door, a delicious aroma of roasting turkey wafted out. It made him feel hungrier than ever.

Sarah was sitting at the table, wearing her angel costume again and eating toast, while Carole was peeling carrots. Jake was asleep in his basket.

"Have we missed breakfast?" Neil asked, dismayed.

"No, I kept yours hot," Carole said. "We thought we'd let you sleep for a bit. You did a marvellous job last night."

"Is Star OK?" Neil said.

"They're all fine," Carole replied. "I gave Star another feed when I got up, and now they're all asleep."

Neil glanced in at the utility room door, and saw Willow curled up peacefully with her pups.

"Can she feed from Willow yet?" he asked.

Carole shook her head. "No, not yet, but I'm sure it's only a matter of time."

Neil wished he felt as confident as his mum. He sat at the kitchen table and helped himself to cereal.

"What did you say to Glen, Dad?" Emily asked. "Did you tell him about the pups?"

"Yes, and he's thrilled," said Bob. "But he's even more thrilled about something else."

Carole looked up sharply from the carrots. "Kate?"

Bob nodded. "Kate had her baby this morning. A little boy. A few days earlier than expected, but they're both fine."

"Brill!" Neil said through a mouthful of cereal. Emily grinned happily.

"I want to see the new baby," Sarah said. "Can we go now?"

"We'll all go to see him," said Carole, "but not today. Kate will be very tired."

"Glen asked me if we'd keep the pups here for a few days," Bob went on. "Just until Kate comes home from hospital. Of course, I said we would. In any case, it's not a good idea to move Star just yet."

"I hope three puppies *and* a baby won't be too

much for Kate," Neil said. "Especially when Star needs so much looking after."

"I'm sure Kate will be happier if Willow's with her," his dad assured him. "I know she's missed her a lot. But we'll have to wait until Star is stronger before they can go home."

"What did Glen say about Star?" Emily asked.

"He was worried, of course. I said I'd leave it to him how much to tell Kate. And we'll keep him up to date with how she's getting on."

Carole brought plates of egg and bacon to the table and set them down in front of Neil and Emily. "You two need a shower to wake you up," she said. "It's Christmas Day and there's a lot to do. How about taking some of the boarding dogs for a walk?"

"Yes!" said Neil. He hesitated and then asked his dad, "Do you think we could take Brutus?"

"Well . . ." Bob stroked his beard. "Maybe if I come with you. He seemed OK first thing when I fed him."

"Great!" Neil attacked his eggs and bacon. "Then we can all see how well he's getting on."

The young Doberman leapt to his feet as Neil went into the rescue centre. He pushed his nose against the mesh to say hello.

"Hi, Brutus," Neil said, slipping him a dog treat. "Fancy a walk?"

He was disappointed to see that Brutus backed off again as Bob came in, but at least he didn't growl.

"He's starting to get used to you," Neil said.

Bob opened the pen door and Neil went in to clip a lead onto Brutus's collar. Then he led Brutus outside.

Snow still lay thickly on the ground. The sky was blue and the sun was shining; it was a perfect day for a walk.

Emily appeared from Kennel Block One with two of the boarding dogs on leads: a Labrador called Cass who was a frequent visitor to King Street and another old friend, a huge mongrel called Bundle. Bob had suggested taking them for a walk with Brutus because they were both reliably good-natured.

As Neil led Brutus across the yard, the Doberman pulled away, as if he was unhappy about being so close to strange dogs. Neil gave him a reassuring pat. "It's OK, boy," he said. "These are friends."

He called to Jake, who was waiting on the back step, and the Border collie bounded down the garden path to the gate which led to the exercise field. His tail waved madly and he let out a joyful bark.

"There," Neil said as he opened the gate. "Go and run the itch out of your feet."

Jake dashed off, snow scattering under his paws as he ran across the field. Brutus pulled on his lead, whining softly, as if he wanted to go after him. *Well!* Neil thought. *He's not scared of Jake!*

"Shall I let him off the lead?" Neil asked.

"OK," said Bob. "But keep a close eye on them."

Neil unclipped the lead and at once Brutus took off after Jake. He leapt up at the Border collie and the two dogs rolled over together in the snow. For a second Neil was anxious, but then he saw that they were just playing, making the most of the snow and the fresh air.

He pulled a ball out of his pocket and threw it. Jake and Brutus raced after it. Jake got there first and, to Neil's relief, Brutus didn't try to fight him for it. He just trotted at Jake's side as Jake brought the ball back to Neil.

"Well done, boys!" Neil said as they came up, slipping them titbits from the supply in his pocket.

Then Bob held out a titbit to Brutus. For a moment it looked as though the big dog would refuse it but Bob spoke to him in a gentle, soothing voice. Slowly, Brutus moved towards Bob's outstretched hand and took the titbit. Bob smiled and so did Neil.

Emily brought Bundle and Cass up for their share and let them off the lead too. Bundle joined in the game with the ball, but Cass was too dignified – or, as Emily said, too lazy!

Neil stood watching the three dogs hurtle across the field. He enjoyed the sight of Brutus's strong, well-muscled body and his shining coat. "Just look at him!" he said proudly. "That's not the same dog we found by the bins. He's learning how to play and to share with other dogs. He deserves a really good home!"

"As soon as Christmas is over," Emily said, "we'll get Jake Fielding to put something in the paper."

"Right," said Neil. He tried to forget about his disappointment that the Meadows family didn't feel able to take the Doberman. "Somewhere there must be somebody who'll realize what a great dog Brutus is!"

Christmas dinner at King Street was as good as it could be. Neil thought his mum cooked the best turkey in the world and his dad's chestnut stuffing was unbeatable!

When the meal was over, everyone went into the sitting-room to open their presents. Neil got a dog encyclopaedia on CD-ROM and Emily had a new Polaroid camera. Sarah's main present was a big box of paints and some animal stencils. Neil had bought special dog treats for Jake and Willow and even Fudge had a new plastic house for his cage.

Emily's eyes shone as she examined her new camera. "I'm going to take pictures of Willow and the pups," she said. "To show Kate, when we go and visit her."

"Good idea," said Carole.

"I think Kate's had the best Christmas presents of anyone," Emily said. "Three puppies and a baby – you can't get much more special than that!"

When the last scrap of Christmas wrapping paper had been cleared away, Bob went out to get on with the kennel work. Even on Christmas Day, the dogs had to be cared for and there was even more to do without Kate and Bev to help.

"We'll come and help, Dad," Emily said. "We'll check on the rescue centre first."

"Remember you're not to go into Brutus's pen," Carole reminded Neil and Emily as they put on warm coats and boots. "I know he's improving, but we still can't be sure he's safe."

Privately Neil thought Brutus would be fine, but he knew better than to argue.

"And I don't know where Sarah's got to," Carole went on. "If she's out there, make sure she's wrapped up well."

"We'll let her cuddle up to a nice, warm dog," Neil promised. "Squirt will love that!"

The sun was already starting to go down

when Neil and Emily went out. The snow in the courtyard was freezing again and icicles hung from the gutters.

There was no sign of Sarah until Neil opened the door of the rescue centre and heard muffled giggling from his little sister. To his amazement, he saw that the door of Brutus's pen was open.

"Squirt!" he exclaimed. "You're not supposed to—"

He stopped, his mouth open in astonishment as he looked inside the pen. Sarah was kneeling down beside Brutus, and she had draped tinsel round his neck and over his head. She was fixing a paper streamer to his collar like a pair of reins.

Brutus just stood still and looked at her. Neil thought he might even be enjoying the attention. His jaws were wide and his tongue lolling out as if he was laughing.

"Just look at that!" he said to Emily.

Sarah looked up. "Brutus is a reindeer," she announced. "He's got long legs so he can go really fast. Next year he's going to pull Father Christmas's sledge."

"Sure, Squirt," Neil said, raising his eyebrows at Emily. "I bet he'll really enjoy that!"

"Neil," Emily said excitedly, "go and get your

camera. This would make a really good picture
for the website!"

Neil grinned. "You're right, it would."

He dashed back to the house and fetched the
digital camera. By the time he got back to the
rescue centre, Emily had helped Sarah to take
off the coat she was wearing over her angel
costume and made her a halo out of tinsel.
Sarah posed with one arm round Brutus's neck
and a huge smile on her face. Brutus's eyes
shone and he was obviously enjoying himself
just as much as Sarah.

"That's perfect!" Neil said. "You know, that
dog has a real sense of humour. He's just never

had the chance to show it."

He took several pictures and all the time Brutus behaved like the friendliest family dog imaginable. When the photocall was finished he came nosing up to Neil, sniffing at his pocket.

"I know what you want," Neil said, fishing out a dog treat. "There – and you deserve it!"

He took the camera straight into the office to put the picture on the website, and Emily went with him, leaving Sarah to take the decorations off Brutus and close up the pen.

"We'll make it the home page picture," Emily said excitedly, "and put 'A Happy Christmas from all at King Street'. It'll show everyone what a great pet Brutus could be."

Neil switched on the computer and downloaded the photos from the digital camera. "I wouldn't let Squirt hear me say this but she looks really cute!" he said.

He had just started writing a caption when he was interrupted by noises from the kitchen. He heard his mother's voice, high in alarm, and then Sarah's, followed by a deep bark.

Neil jumped to his feet. "That's Brutus. Squirt must have brought him into the house!"

Chapter Nine

Neil dashed for the kitchen, with Emily on his heels. It was a rule at King Street that none of the boarding or rescue dogs came into the house. Neil didn't mind the rule being broken, but he guessed his mum would be annoyed, especially if she thought Brutus might be unpredictable.

When he got to the kitchen, Neil saw Brutus standing in the doorway of the utility room, wearing his tinsel reindeer outfit. Sarah was beaming happily, but Carole didn't look so pleased. She had a hand on Jake's collar, restraining him from going over to say hello to the Doberman.

"Neil, thank goodness," Carole said as he

came in. "Take Brutus back to his pen, would you? He shouldn't be in here, he'll disturb Willow."

Sarah's grin vanished. "He likes it here," she objected.

"That's not the point," said Carole. "Willow needs to be kept quiet, and besides, you know the rule. If we start breaking it, we'll be up to our ears in dogs in here."

"Sounds good to me," said Neil. Before Carole could speak, he added hurriedly, "OK, Mum, just coming."

Slowly and calmly, so as not to alarm Brutus, he crossed the kitchen. He knew he had to get the Doberman out of there before he upset Willow, or did anything to harm her litter. Although Brutus was improving all the time, Neil still couldn't be sure that he could be trusted around such tiny pups.

But Brutus showed no sign of being nervous or aggressive. He looked up at Neil with his fine, intelligent eyes and gave a woof, as if he was saying hello.

"Hi, Brutus," Neil said as he reached the dog and gave him a pat.

Inside the utility room, Willow was sitting up in the whelping box, as if she wasn't sure about the intruder. Neil knew how important it was that she shouldn't be disturbed, especially when Star was so weak. He remembered Mike Turner's warning that bitches sometimes attacked their own pups if they were upset. "Steady on, Willow," he said softly.

While Neil stayed beside the Doberman, one hand on the dog's glossy back, Emily went over to Willow and stroked her rough white fur until she settled down again. All the pups were curled up, asleep, and Emily checked to make sure that Star was still breathing. "That's it, girl," she said to Willow as she lay protectively beside the pups. "You take good care of them, you hear?"

While Emily was soothing Willow, Brutus stood motionless in the doorway, looking on with interest. He couldn't have behaved better, Neil thought, and he was clearly not upsetting the other dogs at all.

Then, as Emily was getting up from the whelping box, Neil heard the kitchen door fly open. His dad's voice shouted, "Brutus isn't in his pen!"

Neil's stomach lurched. This loud inter-ruption was the last thing Brutus needed, especially from Bob, who hadn't been the

Doberman's favourite person from the start.

Neil grabbed Brutus's collar, but the Doberman hardly reacted at all, just swinging his head round to see who the newcomer was.

"Well done, boy!" Neil said, patting him. Brutus seemed quite relaxed, not trembling or showing aggression.

"Well!" Bob said. He had halted just inside the back door, and he wasn't looking too pleased. "Was this your idea, Neil?"

"No, it was Sarah," Carole said. "She doesn't understand that Brutus is too highly strung to—"

"Brutus is fine, Mum," Neil protested. "You can see he is."

"He wanted to see the little puppies," said Sarah, looking upset.

"All right, panic over," said Bob. "I thought we'd lost him. Come on, boy, let's put you back where you belong."

"Dad," said Neil, as Bob came over to take the dog, "can't Brutus stay here? Just for now?"

"Now, look, Neil—" Carole began.

"Please!" said Emily. "Brutus has never lived with a proper family. He's never had any fun. And it is Christmas."

"He needs to learn how to be a family dog," Neil added.

Carole was trying to look severe, but her mouth was twitching at the corners. Neil felt hopeful. After all, Brutus hardly looked threatening when he was wearing a pair of tinsel antlers!

"It wouldn't do any harm, just for one evening," Bob said.

"Well, all right," Carole said. Neil let out a cheer and Jake gave an approving bark. "But don't think you can make a habit of it," his mum added. "And keep Brutus well out of the way while you're feeding Star."

"Sure, Mum," said Neil.

Neil unwound Brutus's decorations, and then he and Emily took him into the office while they finished updating the website. The big dog sat quietly beside them, his ears pricked.

"Do you like your picture, Brutus?" Emily asked.

The Doberman gave the computer screen a long look and then let out a bark.

"Is that a yes or a no?" asked Neil.

"It must be a yes," said Emily. "That's the best home page picture we've ever had!"

Neil switched off the computer and led the

way into the sitting-room, where Sarah and Bob
were watching *The Wizard of Oz*. Brutus padded
after Neil and Emily and flopped down at Bob's
feet as if he had been living with them all his
life.

When the film ended, Carole called Neil and
Emily into the kitchen to give Star her evening
feed. They left Brutus snoozing with Jake in
front of the sitting-room fire.

While Carole fed Willow in the utility room,
Neil brought Star into the kitchen and cuddled
her on his lap. He loved the feel of her soft white
fur, all fluffed up from Willow's tongue. He was
trying hard to convince himself that the tiny

pup was growing stronger, but when he compared Star to her brother and sister he had to admit there was a long way to go.

Emily held the feeding bottle and both she and Neil watched anxiously as Star weakly sucked the milk.

"Do you want to do the night feeds again?" Bob asked, turning from the sink where he was washing up. "I'll take over if you like."

"No, we can manage, Dad," Neil said. "I want to—"

He broke off as the kitchen door swung open. Brutus appeared in the doorway and before anyone could move he trotted across the kitchen and pushed his nose into Neil's lap, where Star lay.

Neil couldn't help feeling a jolt of alarm. Brutus's head was bigger than the whole of Star's body and he had a lot of teeth. He could swallow the tiny pup with no trouble if he wanted to!

"Brutus!" Emily gasped.

Then Neil saw that they had all been wrong not to trust Brutus, even for a moment. The big dog nosed Star affectionately and his tongue rasped along her coat.

As Star felt the gentle licking she gave a

wriggle and let out a tiny squeak. Neil had never seen her respond like that before.

"Hey!" He grinned broadly, feeling a surge of hope for the tiny pup. "It's as if Brutus knows that Star is feeling poorly!"

Bob came over to have a look. "You've done a good job with Brutus," he said approvingly. "He's settled down into a lovely dog. The family who gets him will be very lucky."

Neil glowed inside. It looked like Brutus was having a happy Christmas after all.

After lunch on Boxing Day, the Parkers got ready to visit Kate in hospital. Brutus had been put back into his pen the night before but Neil had taken him out for a run in the exercise field with Jake that morning.

"Mum," Sarah said excitedly, "I want to take Willow and the puppies to show Kate. Can we?"

Carole was packing up some magazines for Kate and a soft woolly dog for the new baby. "I'm afraid not," she said gently. "The nurses would never let them into the hospital."

Sarah's mouth drooped. "But Kate will *want* to see them."

"Don't worry," said Emily. She waved an envelope and tucked it into the pocket of her coat. "I took lots of photographs with my new camera. Specially so Kate can see Willow and the pups."

"And Brutus!" said Neil.

In the hospital, Kate was sitting by the side of her bed, wearing a pretty quilted dressing gown. Glen was there, too, grinning from ear to ear as the Parkers peered into the cradle beside the bed.

"Oh, he's *gorgeous*!" exclaimed Carole. "What have you called him?"

"Noel," said Kate. "Because he was born on Christmas Day."

The baby looked very small and crumpled.

He was wrapped up in a white blanket and his eyes were tightly closed.

"Look, Kate," said Emily, pulling out the envelope full of photographs. "I took these for you."

Kate laid out the pictures on her bed, exclaiming over Willow and the pups.

"We called that one Angel," Neil told her, pointing to the biggest pup. "And that one is Tinsel."

"And the little one is Star," Emily added. "But if you don't like those names you can change them."

"I wouldn't dream of it," said Kate. "They're perfect names for Christmas pups. Thank you! All of you – for looking after them all so well. I don't know what I would have done without you."

"All part of the Puppy Patrol service," said Bob, smiling.

"Isn't Star small?" Sarah said, examining one of the pictures. "She's the littlest puppy I've ever seen."

"How is she?" Kate asked anxiously. Glen had obviously told her that Star was very weak.

"I'm sure she'll be fine," Carole reassured her. "Neil and Emily have been feeding her every two hours and she's holding her own."

Kate smiled, trying to look brave, but Neil could see she was still worried. Kate knew just as much about dogs as they did; she would understand that Star wouldn't be out of danger until she could feed from her mum.

"You should have seen Brutus!" he said, hoping to distract Kate. "He really loves Star."

Kate picked up one of the pictures that showed the young Doberman. In the photograph, Brutus was sitting beside Neil, looking down protectively at Star as she lay in Neil's lap.

"He's a fabulous dog," said Glen. His voice was full of admiration.

"He certainly is," Bob agreed. "Little Star has a friend for life."

"Have you managed to find a home for Brutus yet?" Glen asked.

Neil shook his head. "We're going to make a big effort as soon as the holiday is over. We might get Jake Fielding to do an article about him in the *Compton News*."

"Don't worry, somebody will want him," Glen said, fingering the picture thoughtfully. "In fact, you know, we—"

"Glen Paget!" Kate interrupted, laughing. "I

112

know what you're thinking. We just haven't got space for a new baby, Willow and her pups *and* a big dog like Brutus."

"I suppose you're right." Glen put the picture down regretfully.

Neil felt a rush of disappointment, although he couldn't help agreeing. He thought the Pagets would be great owners for Brutus, but he knew Kate would have enough to cope with already when she went home. *But somewhere,* Neil thought, *there's a family waiting to give a great home to Brutus. All I have to do is find them!*

Chapter Ten

As Bob turned the King Street Kennels' Range Rover into the drive, Neil saw an unfamiliar car parked there.

"Who can that be?" Carole asked. "I told everybody we were closed over Christmas Day and Boxing Day."

The Range Rover had hardly come to a stop when the door of the car burst open and Jackie Meadows scrambled out.

"Neil! Neil!" She dashed over to him as he got out of the Range Rover. "We've come for Brutus!"

Neil was so dazed for a moment that he could hardly take in what she was telling him.

Jackie grabbed his shoulders and gave him a

shake. "Brutus!" she repeated. "He is still here, isn't he? Nobody's come to take him?"

Neil suddenly grasped what Jackie was saying. He felt a big bubble of happiness expanding inside him. "No," he managed to say. "He's still here."

"He's waiting for you," Emily said. She was grinning widely. "He's been your dog all along."

Mr and Mrs Meadows followed Jackie across the yard and shook hands with Bob and Carole. "We really didn't feel we could risk Brutus with our twins at first," Mr Meadows said. "They can be pretty lively and they might startle Brutus without meaning to."

"And then we saw the picture on your website," Mrs Meadows continued. "That lovely photograph of Brutus with your little girl. It's quite plain he's good with children. So we talked it over and—"

"And we decided to have him!" Jackie finished. Anxiously she added, "We can have him, can't we?"

"I can't think of anyone better," Carole told her, smiling, while Neil said, "You bet!"

"I'm sorry to disturb you on Boxing Day," Mrs Meadows went on, "but Jackie insisted on coming over right away. My mum and dad are at home with Ben and Nicky. I didn't want to overwhelm Brutus!"

"Can we take him now?" Jackie asked eagerly.

"Of course you can," said Carole. "Bob, if you take them over to the rescue centre, I'll go into the office and sort out the paperwork."

She let herself into the house while the rest of the Parkers led the Meadows family through the side gate and into the rescue centre.

Brutus leapt up as soon as he saw Jackie and padded up to the front of the pen. Neil opened the door for her. She went in, knelt down and flung her arms round Brutus.

"You're ours!" she said. "You're really ours!"

Her parents stood looking down at them, smiling, while Brutus licked her face enthusiastically. His stumpy tail was wagging vigorously. Neil and Emily exchanged a satisfied nod. There was nothing they liked better than matching up a dog with an owner who would give it the best possible home.

"I have to say that you're getting a wonderful dog," Bob told Mr and Mrs Meadows. "A Doberman is one of the bravest and most faithful dogs around."

"Do you hear that, Brutus?" Jackie

whispered. She leant closer to him, as if she was sharing a secret. "I knew you were perfect!"

"I see from the website that you hold obedience classes," Mr Meadows said.

"That's right," said Bob. "Sunday mornings and Wednesday evenings."

"Then I think we'd better book Brutus in for a course," said Mr Meadows. "He's had a bad start, but I'm sure he'll soon learn."

"I'll bring him," Jackie said, looking up with her face glowing. "You'd like that, wouldn't you, boy?"

Brutus gave a loud woof, and planted a paw on her knee.

"I think we can call that a yes," said Neil.

*

While Mr and Mrs Meadows filled out forms with Carole in the office, Neil and Emily took Jackie and Brutus into the kitchen. It was time for Star's next feed. Neil made up the milk formula while Jackie and Emily went to look at Willow's pups.

When he took the feeding bottle into the utility room, he found Jackie sitting on the floor with Tinsel on her lap. Sarah was cuddling Angel, while Emily gently cradled Star. Brutus nosed his tiny friend and gave her another lick. Willow had left the whelping box to have a drink and say hello to Jake. Neil was relieved to see that she looked quite calm about all the human and doggy visitors.

"Do you really have to feed Star every two hours?" Jackie asked. "In the night as well?"

"In the night as well," Emily confirmed.

"That's right," said Neil. "For as long as she needs us."

After all the excitement, he was just beginning to realize how sleepy he was feeling. He wasn't looking forward to another disturbed night, but he was determined not to share Star's care with anyone but Emily. They had promised Mike that they would be responsible for her and they would see it through.

Neil held the feeding bottle to Star's lips but, to his dismay, she refused to suck. Even Carole's trick of letting her lick milk from his fingers didn't work this time. Star made tiny mewing noises and scrabbled her paws against Emily's hands, but every time Neil tried to give her the bottle she turned her head away.

"What's the matter with her?" Emily asked desperately. "She was fine earlier on. She can't give up now, she just can't!"

Sarah looked up from petting Angel, her lip quivering.

"She's *got* to feed," Neil said determinedly. He couldn't bear to think that after all their efforts Star might not survive. "Come on, midget – lovely milk!"

Very gently he tried to guide Star's head towards the bottle, but she wriggled away before he could get the teat into her mouth. Neil let out a frustrated sigh.

"What are you going to do?" Jackie asked.

"Tell Dad," said Emily. She handed Star over to Neil. "I'll go and fetch him."

Brutus gave Star a tiny lick, as if he felt just as worried as Neil. Neil stroked the little pup's fuzzy white fur and put her back in the whelping box beside Willow, who was just settling down again.

Star gave a wriggle and cuddled up close to her mum. Then, to Neil's utter astonishment, she took one of Willow's teats into her mouth and began to suck.

Neil stared. "She's doing it!" he whispered. "She's feeding properly!"

"Oh, wow!" said Jackie.

"Hooray!" shouted Sarah.

At that moment, Emily came back into the utility room with Bob. Neil waved urgently to warn them to keep still and they both stood in the doorway, watching the tiny pup as she sucked blissfully.

"No wonder she didn't want the bottle," said Neil. "It's a pretty poor substitute for the real thing!"

"Will Star be OK now?" Emily asked Bob.

"I'm sure she will," her dad replied. "That was the big hurdle – to get her feeding from her mum. We'll keep an eye on her, obviously, but I don't think there's anything to worry about any more."

"And no more getting up in the middle of the night!" Neil said with relief. "You know what?" he added to Jackie. "I reckon Brutus helped Star to get better too."

120

"Really?"

"Really. Brutus seemed to know that Star was weaker than the others, and he always paid extra attention to her."

Jackie put her arms round Brutus and gave him a hug. "You're the best, Brutus! I always knew it."

Neil heard the door from the hall opening, and voices in the kitchen. "That's your mum and dad," he said to Jackie. "We'd better go. It's bad for Willow to have too many people in here."

Reluctantly he tore his eyes away from little Star and led the way into the kitchen. Carole was explaining to Mr and Mrs Meadows about the diet sheets she'd given them for Brutus.

"Mum," Neil said, "Star's feeding from Willow!"

Carole's face lit up with relief and happiness. "At last! That's wonderful news."

Jackie was bubbling over with excitement, telling her mum and dad how Neil and Emily had been looking after Star.

"I'm certainly impressed with what I've seen here," said Mr Meadows, shaking Bob's hand.

"We do our best," said Bob, smiling.

"Little Star probably wouldn't be here without you," said Jackie. "And I wouldn't have

Brutus. I think you're all great!"

Neil felt himself starting to go red. "Oh, well," he said, "that's what we do. If there's a dog in trouble, just send for the Puppy Patrol!"

PUPPY PATROL® titles available from
Macmillan Children's Books

The prices shown below are correct at the time of going to press.
However, Macmillan Publishers reserve the right to show new retail
prices on covers which may differ from those previously advertised.

JENNY DALE

1.	Teacher's Pet	£3.50	22.	Superdog!	£3.50
2.	Big Ben	£3.50	23.	Sherlock's Home	£3.50
3.	Abandoned!	£3.50	24.	Forever Sam	£3.50
4.	Double Trouble	£3.50	25.	Milly's Triumph	£3.50
5.	Star Paws	£3.50	26.	The Snow Dog	£3.50
6.	Tug of Love	£3.50	27.	Boomerang Bob	£3.50
7.	Saving Skye	£3.50	28.	Willow's Wood	£3.50
8.	Tuff's Luck	£3.50	29.	Dognapped!	£3.50
9.	Red Alert	£3.50	30.	Puppy Power!	£3.50
10.	The Great Escape	£3.50	31.	Two's Company	£3.50
11.	Perfect Puppy	£3.50	32.	Digger's Treasure	£3.50
12.	Sam & Delilah	£3.50	33.	Homeward Bound	£3.50
13.	The Sea Dog	£3.50	34.	The Puppy Express	£3.50
14.	Puppy School	£3.50	35.	Holly's Wish	£3.50
15.	A Winter's Tale	£3.50	36.	Barney's Rescue	£3.50
16.	Puppy Love	£3.50	37.	Lost and Found	£3.50
17.	Best of Friends	£3.50	38.	Top Dog!	£3.50
18.	King of the Castle	£3.50	39.	Stars and Stripes	£3.50
19.	Posh Pup	£3.50	40.	Husky Hero	£3.50
20.	Charlie's Choice	£3.50	41.	Trick or Treat?	£3.50
21.	The Puppy Project	£3.50	42.	Little Star	£3.50

All Macmillan titles can be ordered at your local bookshop
or are available by post from:

**Book Service by Post
PO Box 29, Douglas, Isle of Man IM99 1BQ**

Credit cards accepted. For details:
Telephone: 01624 675137
Fax: 01624 670923
E-mail: bookshop@enterprise.net

Free postage and packing in the UK.
Overseas customers: add £1 per book (paperback)
and £3 per book (hardback).